I0594693

ABOUT THE AUTHOR

Kellie M Cox is an Australian writer indulging her love of fiction and prose. With qualifications in psychology, she relishes writing about the human condition and the vulnerability of the psyche. A therapist, clinical trainer, creative coach and conservationist, she enjoys a dream life on the beautiful Gold Coast.

Wanting to see a change in the narrative of gender roles in storytelling, Kellie has created her publishing and production enterprise, Strong Female Protagonists and encourages others to write and produce work that challenges our preconceived ideas of societal values.

Most days Kellie can be found working with artists in the creative industries or writing her novels. When not writing, Kellie will likely be saturating her social media accounts with photos of her adorable dogs.

Follow Kellie on social media as KellieCoxWriter and KellieMCox.

www.kelliemcox.com
www.strongfemaleprotagonists.com

WRITTEN BY KELLIE M COX

Fiction
Murderous Intent (2019)
The List (2020)
The Reef (2020)
The Last First Kiss (2021)

Non-Fiction
Advice For Life (2021)

Short Stories
Death by Trident (2018)
Short Yarns for Big Imaginations, GCWA.

The Last First Kiss

KELLIE M COX

Strong Female Protagonists

The Last First Kiss

Published by Kellie M Cox
and

www.KellieMCox.com
www.StrongFemaleProtagonists.com

ISBN 978 0 6484767 6 4 (paperback)
ISBN 978 0 6484767 7 1 (ebook)
Author - Kellie M Cox
Graphic Design – Elloise Sullivan
Cover Design - Blair Renwick
Logo and Website Design – Connor Renwick

DEDICATION

To Blair and Connor, this dedication is for you. I loved you long before I met you. I will love you forever more. Spend your lives creating moments and you will never regret a day of your life.

ONE

Piazza Barberini, Rome

Twilight transformed the Piazza Barberini. Late afternoon and the lights began to glow under the eclectic mix of old and new infrastructure surrounding the glorious Fontana del Tritone. The magnificent statue of Triton, son of Neptune took centre stage in the cobbled square. The proud figure depicted Triton himself stopping the great flood with the sounding of his horn. The beauty and strength of the artwork had been admired in Rome since its creation in 1643. Old in Rome meant ancient, with the history of this city proudly on display for centuries.

The statue itself dated back to the family Barberini, the wealthy Roman family said to be known for borrowing or recycling valuable archeological treasures after the fall of their beloved city. So famous was the family that the very square was dedicated to their name. A well-known saying in Rome was, whatever the Barbarians didn't take, the Barberinis probably did. The ancient surrounds suited this particular outing more than any other Samantha had undertaken during her month long stay in Italy.

Readying herself to commence the much-anticipated tour of the crypts and catacombs of early Rome, Samantha headed for the designated meeting place next to the statue of Triton. A glance at her phone suggested enough time for a quick snack before the tour organiser was to meet them. She headed across the busy street to her now favourite cafe. Ordering a baguette with tomato and mozzarella cheese, Samantha was quickly on her way again and outside once more to gather with the crowds in the paved square.

She chose a seat against the edge of the fountain as she watched the other tourists around her enjoying the sights and sounds of Rome on sunset. She heard a voice with an American accent politely declining the offer of fresh roses from a street vendor. The family seated next to her watched on with surprise as the vendor ignored the polite decline and dropped a bunch of pink roses on the hapless tourist's lap. The tourist smiled politely and thanked the vendor, obviously uncomfortable with the unwanted attention from the stranger.

"Watch what he does now," the teenage girl from the family group next to Samantha demanded of her parents. "He will stand there and wait for money." The family watched on, as did Samantha. Unfortunately, Samantha had seen it all before many times over.

True to the script, the vendor started pleading with the tourist in his broken English, "Please, you help me out. We are friends. You help me out a little."

Wanting the spectacle to come to an end, the tourist handed back the flowers once more. This time, the vendor seeing another victim to attend to, snatched the flowers and marched away.

The sideshow had distracted them all from the tour coordinator who had arrived to perform her arbitrary task of checking tourists' names from her preprinted list. Samantha stepped into line, placing the remains of her baguette into the bin as she did. She had been ravenous moments earlier, but only a few small bites had managed to fill her sufficiently.

The organiser looked up from her folder. Samantha knew the drill and gave her name. "Samantha Cleary," she informed the eager tour coordinator who found her name without delay and tore a round, green sticker from the roll as she asked Samantha to place it on herself.

"Please make your way across the street and join the green group. You will meet your guide there."

Samantha had never been one for organised tours, in fact there was nothing she despised more than having to load on and off buses with dozens of other travellers, jostling for space to strain to hear every last word of the knowledgeable guides so as to not miss an essential fact.

Samantha headed toward the group and recognised already some of the crowd who had earlier gathered at the statue, including the harassed American tourist who had refused to purchase the roses from the street vendor. Individuals smiled sweetly at each other, knowing that with time they would be chattering amongst themselves like long lost friends. That was the skill of the successful guide, to entertain a group while introducing them to each other and the marvels of the new world they had come to visit.

Samantha glanced over at an odd-looking pair sitting on a step not far from the group. An elderly woman, possibly of European descent and a bearded man in a leather jacket, maybe mid-thirties she guessed. The man immediately glanced up at Samantha as if he had felt her stare.

Her throat caught. Those eyes, those familiar eyes. She felt foolish for staring and mortified for getting caught in the act but she couldn't wrench her glare away from his face. He smiled at her and Samantha erupted in an involuntary grin.

There was no running away and hiding for Samantha. The man in the black jacket leapt from the step, as he uttered a quick word of farewell to his older companion and made his way directly toward Samantha's group.

"Hello, green group. I am your guide. My name is David," he began by way of introduction to his tour group for the night.

Samantha's shoulders fell back as her spine straightened. David had captured her full attention. She was to spend the next four hours or so in the company of these strangers, and she couldn't be more pleased. She smiled to herself for shamelessly ogling their attractive guide and getting caught in the act of doing it. She hoped he had a good sense of humour about it.

Samantha just couldn't help herself. She stood by hopelessly mesmerised by his voice; deep, commanding and in control but at the same time light and entertaining. The accent, American she guessed, although flecked with something a little difficult to detect. David made his way around the group who had now begun to form a neat, small singular circle around him. Samantha watched him make his way toward her. She couldn't divert her stare from him. His mouth now smiling as he personally greeted each and every traveller by shaking their hand and asking pertinent details about where they were from and how long they had been travelling through Italy.

Samantha was standing only three tourists away from meeting the gorgeous David for herself. She dared not glare too long but she couldn't resist. She tried to look away and pretended to stare at the ground beneath her. He stood directly in front of her. She glanced up to see first his beautiful full lips, followed by his enchanting smile and then the eyes. Oh, those eyes, a deep and complicated mix of hazel green. They sparkled. The eyes, she somehow knew those eyes.

"Hi, I'm David from California." He raised his hand to her and Samantha lifted hers to join him. He brought his other forearm over to completely cover her hand with both of his. Samantha felt the heaviness in her chest. She realised she was holding her breath. David smiled down at her, obviously in no rush to move on.

"And your name is?" he encouraged her to introduce herself to him.

"I'm Samantha," she stammered. And in reply, David made the most unusual and unexplained gesture. He slowly tilted his head back as if looking skyward as he closed his eyes for just a moment. Samantha felt at the same time his hands over hers tighten. They felt warm, comforting and strangely familiar. There was nothing uneasy about their physical contact, even though there was every reason for discomfort with this absolute stranger.

David let out a breath into the frosty European winter. Samantha watched the warm of his exhale as it made that delightful white puff of mist as the heat from his breath meet with the cold night air. Samantha couldn't fathom what was happening. David slowly lowered his head to meet her eyes once more. His smile, wide and glistening made her grin as well. He spoke softly and deliberately.

"I knew a Samantha once," he chuckled a little as the words left his mouth.

Samantha felt indignant. She didn't quite know what he meant by his vague comment and wasn't sure she entirely desired to hear more.

"Are you from Australia, Sam?" David quickly added.

"Yes, Queensland actually," she was purposefully vague in her response. "And it's Samantha actually. Nobody has called me Sam since I was a child."

His smile lit up once more. His eyes widened as he pulled her joined palms toward him which in turn forced his body even closer to hers.

"I knew a Samantha from Australia once," he laughed again to himself as he finally released his hold on her hands and began to make his way toward the young couple to her left.

Samantha was quick to reply before he moved away completely. "I knew a David once too." She paused and reflected a moment to herself before adding, "But that was a very long time ago."

David returned to her once more, standing directly in front of her as he spoke again. "I bet you did, Sam." His cheeky comment was nothing short of pure foreplay. She was sure of it. Samantha hadn't always been the best at picking up on a man's flirtations but there was no denying this man was doing his best to get her attention.

David moved on and greeted the final of his tour guests for the night. Samantha felt absolutely unnerved. Her body was tingling from head to toe. A younger version of herself would most likely exit quietly from the group at this point to sneak into the falling darkness and the busy crowds of Rome. But not the thirty-four-year-old version of Samantha. She was looking forward to flirting with this handsome stranger that the universe had delivered directly to her.

David turned to command his group, "Ok, let's go green group. Everyone got a partner? I won't ever leave a man, woman or child behind. Partner up as we make our way through the dark tunnels of the catacombs. Make sure you have your travel buddy with you at all times. Everyone good?"

Samantha stood alone, slightly embarrassed to admit that she didn't have a partner. One of the only negatives of travelling alone was the odd occasion such as this when she really needed to have a companion with her. David caught her eye and spoke to the group again.

"Looks like everyone but Sam here has a partner. So, I will watch out for Sam. Green group let's go! Follow me! Come on Sam, partner up!" he encouraged her.

Samantha didn't need any further encouragement to take the few steps she needed to walk toward David. The opportunity to be closer to him and the idea that this gorgeous specimen of a man was going to look out for her was all the enticement she needed to continue. Samantha rallied in with the rest of the group behind David, not too close but not too far away from her travel buddy. She stayed just near enough to ensure she didn't get lost.

Throughout the ride to the site the tourists were enthralled by the knowledge David shared of the history they passed at every corner. The wealth of information stored in his brain was impressive. Samantha wondered how the Californian came to be in Rome and leading tours of the city's ancient ruins. On arriving at the site, Samantha was reminded once more to stay close. Each person found their travel buddy and walked slowly down the long stairs that led to the burial ground of tens of thousands of Romans.

The stark temperature drop was evidence of their travel far underground. The absence of the last remnants of daylight proved an eerie setting for this particularly morbid tour. As the group followed close by to each other, it became apparent that one wrong turn when down in this sacred ground could prove to be a fatal error. No signs suggested the way, no map was provided. With skills and obvious experience navigating this landscape, David led his followers through one turn after another, stopping frequently to add vital details to the rich history of the story of the Roman catacombs.

The walk through the dark tunnels of the catacombs was beyond description. Without taking photos, which was her great passion, Samantha was forced to take in each and every step. The history and stories behind these ancient burial grounds had her mesmerised. It was saddening to think of so many lives lost, but at the same time incredible that this historical record was kept and preserved for future generations to visit.

"Is that a human bone?" the teenager with the family from London asked David. He glanced over, quite unaffected by the question and informed the group that indeed there were still some human remains down in the catacombs but for the most part each person had been moved to a new and final resting ground.

As is human nature, each traveller took a moment to glance over the small railing to see what appeared to be a human femur bone. Samantha was the last in line and she lingered for a second to imagine to whom this bone may have once belonged. A rather morbid thought for some but the idea of death didn't frighten Samantha. Instead she had unfortunately become acquainted with death, and from that had learnt the value of life and of time. More particularly, not wasting time. Which of course was the very reason she found herself that night in Rome.

Having loved travel from a very early age, Samantha didn't resist any opportunity to explore a new city. She had lots of time to use and a little money saved up. She had looked at the world map on her office wall to determine which country she should explore next. She decided she had time to spare, so she picked up her trusty fluorescent highlighter pen and put a big pink dot on Europe. She immediately booked a flight to Rome and that was the most detailed as her simple and easy planning had been.

With the goal of doing some blogging while travelling, Samantha had hoped she would realise her life-long dream of being a full-time traveller, exploring the world and writing about her adventures. She had gained some initial royalties from a publishing imprint executive who encouraged her to travel and write, with the view that her blogs could in time become a book series which would allow her the mobile income to explore the entire world.

Lost in her thoughts, she was startled by a strong hand on the small of her back as David leaned in to check on her.

"Are you ok Sam?" He seemed concerned.

"Yes, it is just overwhelming isn't it? I never imagined there were so many people buried down here," she replied.

David was quick to respond. His concern for her appeared to be heightened. "Do you want me to take you back up?"

The reality of the situation was that there was no way that a first timer would ever find their way back through the maze of tunnels that formed this ancient burial ground and navigate the hundreds of stairs that lead back up to the surface.

"No, no I am fine. I am enjoying it, really I am," Samantha responded.

Samantha quickly realised she had been holding up the group and that David had come back for her alone. She felt shocked at her lack of awareness but also a little excited to be standing alone with David. She looked up into his eyes and said, "I'm sorry. Please let's get back to the group. I apologise for making you come back and get me."

David just smiled as he reached down, took her hand in his and led her back to the group, safely and patiently waiting at the next crypt for David and his lost travel buddy.

David released her hand as he positioned her at the front of the group. He took his place once more as the centre of the travellers' attention.

"I have Sam!" he informed the group. "I will repeat my earlier warning. Remember, stay close to your travel buddy. I won't leave a man, woman or child behind down here." He stared directly into Samantha's eyes. The corners of his mouth turned upright in a knowing smile.

The group laughed at his lighthearted humour, which masked a very real safety warning. Samantha, oblivious to his words lifted her hand to look at it. It was tingling from his touch, so much so she fully expected to see her palm bright red with the heat of a burn on her delicate skin.

"And besides, it wouldn't be a very pleasant night down here all alone, would it now Sam?" David interjected her thoughts once more as he continued to emphasise the importance of his warning to the tour group.

She looked up and smiled at him. She wondered if there was some greater meaning to his reference to spending a night alone? She bit her bottom lip at the thought of it. She imagined with his looks, wit and intelligence, this wasn't a man who was ever forced to spend a night alone if he was in need of company. She was determined to find out if indeed alone he was. She wouldn't mind at all, more of his company whilst in the romantic city of Rome.

TWO

Rome, Italy

At the end of the tour, the walk to the top of the stairs left Samantha slightly out of breath. She was glad that for once David wasn't right beside her. She was already in her third decade of life but had still failed to nail down any real exercise regime. Sure, she was happy to hit the gym with friends from time to time. She had enjoyed the hot yoga experience and even didn't mind a good boxing workout occasionally. But to say that she was diligent about her workout or exercise was an overstatement.

Samantha headed for the bathroom, not necessarily because she needed to but because she desperately wanted a quiet place to capture her thoughts for a moment. She was finding the evening more and more interesting but also more bewildering as the night drew on. She recognised within herself an astonishing feeling that she hadn't felt for a very long time. She felt sparks. She actually felt some very real attraction to the handsome man that was their tour guide for the evening. She wondered for a second if they had some ethical code like a doctor or therapist, which meant he couldn't date a member of his tour group.

She stopped herself from jumping straight ahead again. She had a knack of doing exactly that. She knew she had an instant attraction to David, but at the same time, who wouldn't? He was gorgeous, knowledgeable and funny and he was also showing signs of real compassion and care. He demonstrated empathy for the tour group members but also for the real histories of the people whose graves they had just visited. Those people, whose stories needed to be told with respect and humanity for their lives now long gone.

She headed straight to the first available cubicle, closed and locked the door behind herself.

"What the hell is going on?" she asked herself out loud. She sighed a loud sigh and closed her eyes tightly.

"Is everything ok in there?" the familiar British accent from the mother in the tour group enquired.

She giggled at being caught talking to herself inside the toilet cubicle. "Yes, thanks. I'm fine, just a little bit of self-talk," Samantha politely answered the concerned visitor.

"You must do that a lot, travelling alone and all," the middle-aged motherly voice of concern from the cubicle next to her added.

Samantha sighed, but silently and to herself this time. "Yes, yes I guess so," she replied. She couldn't take offence. How could she really? This woman, old enough to be her own mother was just showing concern for a younger female traveller's wellbeing.

Both women made their way from the cubicles to the sinks. The British mother now feeling very familiar with Samantha, most likely as a result of having a conversation through a toilet cubicle wall as women do, had more insight to share.

"That David hey? He's a bit of a dish, isn't he?" the woman announced without provocation.

Samantha grinned from ear to ear, pleased that she wasn't the only one to notice. "He is, isn't he," she wholeheartedly admitted. She wasn't the least bit concerned about giving too much away to the stranger too quickly.

"And he seems to have taken quite a shine to you, hasn't he?" the woman continued.

The warmth returned to Samantha's skin. Even the cold night air coming through the bathroom opening didn't cool the heat that she felt rising in her face. She was glad to think that someone else had noticed the attention too. This provided the confirmation she needed that she wasn't reading too much into his shameless flirting.

"But he seems a bit handsy for me, love. You know, for someone you've just met. He can't seem to keep his hands off you." Samantha had noticed the woman travelling with a teenage girl, who she assumed to be her daughter and imagined that as a mother of a teenager she probably had some very strong views about how women should be treated.

"You have just met him, haven't you?" The mother thought to check her assumption, before sharing any further opinions of their gorgeous tour guide.

Samantha stopped for a moment before answering. She had wondered exactly that. Those eyes, those eyes were all too familiar to her, but she had no idea why. She couldn't recall meeting David before but for some reason she felt completely and utterly comfortable around him. It was a little disconcerting but a surprisingly pleasant feeling to have.

"I must admit he seems familiar, but no we hadn't met before tonight. Not before he introduced himself to each of us in the Piazza Barberini."

The two women made their way from the bathroom area and toward David and the waiting group. Samantha's new friend made the group first, proudly announcing to all, "I've got Samantha!" The group laughed at Samantha being the centre of attention once more and the obvious butt of their jokes for the night.

David looked sheepishly at her as he mouthed the word, "Sorry." At least, Samantha thought, he had some realisation of the unwanted attention he was causing her for his own and the groups' amusement.

The next stop for the tour group was the ancient church in the centre of Rome, concealing beneath it centuries upon centuries of history. An historical lasagna, as the Romans called it. Ancient buildings destroyed through war or ruin crushed and packed down to act as the foundation for the next layer of building works. Clever architects of design were able to determine which ancient structures would provide the greatest strength to hold the enormous buildings that would now take pride of place in the new Rome.

Samantha watched as David's animated storytelling challenged the groups' existing views of Catholicism. Suggesting that all religions were basically the same, David was respectful but unforgiving in the delivery of this serious message. This was a man who knew not only his adopted city of Rome and its centuries of history, but someone who also demonstrated a vast depth and breadth of knowledge in religion and philosophy. Samantha could stand and listen to him talk for hours.

It was at that pivotal and meaningful moment in David's speech that Samantha felt her throat tickle and the inevitable cough that she knew would follow, barked from her mouth. She tried desperately to be quiet by covering her mouth with the bulk of her scarf. She had no idea why this kept happening. It had started on the plane to Italy and had continued each day she had been in the colder climate. She knew once it started she needed to have a drink of water to ease the dryness in her throat.

David continued, seemingly unnerved by the distraction of her coughing. He took several steps toward her at the end of the semi -circle the group had formed around him and raised his hand to her. Samantha put her hand out and David dropped a small something wrapped in paper into her palm. Without thinking, without even looking at what it might be, Samantha unwrapped the small hard item and placed it in her mouth.

She began to suck on the menthol lozenge as David turned to her once more, without faltering, without skipping a word of his well-practiced speech and gave her a knowing wink.

It was a small gesture that meant so very much. He hadn't registered any annoyance at her coughing. He had barely acknowledged the disturbing sound as he addressed the group. He was completely attuned to her and she to him. She felt so safe in his presence that she didn't even question or look at what he had given her. She just unwrapped the offering and knew exactly what to do with it. Samantha had never felt this level of comfort with a man before. This knowing, this sensing what each other was thinking was exhilarating for her.

More narrow corridors and many more steps followed the second venue of the evening tour. A quick dash through the narrow streets to the waiting bus found Samantha once more at the back of the group. Walking through the rear entrance of the bus and finding a seat to herself in the empty rows, she quickly settled in for a pleasant drive to their final destination.

David was at the lead again at the front of the bus. "Ok, do we have everyone? Everyone got his or her partner? Where's mine?" He glanced around the bus. Samantha felt herself sit up in her seat.

"Where's Sam?" David asked once more, this time with a slight hint of panic rising in his voice as he began to fear that he might have inadvertently left his tour buddy behind.

Samantha raised her hand and responded with enthusiasm, "Here I am."

"There you are beautiful." The words were out of his mouth before he even realised what he had said.

"Oh!" the British mother, Samantha's new best friend from the bathroom called out. The rest of the group laughed awkwardly. Some of the women giggled with embarrassment for Samantha. Most appeared envious of the attention she was receiving from their handsome guide.

All Samantha could do was to smile a wide smile in return. She secretly wished this night would never end but she knew that within just another hour or so the tour would be over.

Everyone finally settled into their seats as David took the microphone to announce to the group the important landmarks as they passed each. Samantha did what she loved doing most and grabbed her camera to take some photos where she could of the passing sights. She knew that none of the photos would be in focus but the familiarity and comfort of the camera in front of her face had become second nature to her now during her travels.

She was pleasantly distracted aiming out of the window of the bus when she felt him sit down beside her. He was quick to say what he had come to say.

"Sam, I am so sorry. I didn't mean to embarrass you by calling you that. I don't know how the word slipped out of my mouth."

She looked into his eyes and then directly at his mouth as he whispered the words for just her to hear. She imagined herself leaning forward and placing her lips on his. Needing no words, just the intense desire to touch him. She was in a trancelike state when he asked, "Will you forgive me please?"

"David…" she began, but it was too late.

The bus had pulled to a halt and without further a word David was up from his seat beside her, addressing the waiting crowd once more, "Ok, now green group this is our final stop for the night, so don't leave anything on the bus. Take your buddy and meet me in the lobby of that building."

David pointed toward the old church in front of them. It seemed no different to the hundreds of churches that Rome housed. The steep stairs that led to the entrance of the building not giving any hint as to the hidden wonders beneath the Church of Santa Maria della Concezione dei Cappuccini.

Samantha gathered her camera, backpack and jacket and made her way down the rear stairs of the bus. David quickly joined her, placing his hand on the small of her back once more. The warm sensation of his palm on her body was tantalisingly arousing.

"David…" Samantha began again to ask the question on the tip of her tongue, finding the moment to finally ask, "Have we… met before?"

She couldn't help but to ask the question searing through her mind. The possibility of a previous meeting, the only answer for this surprising sense of connection between the two strangers. It seemed an obvious question, not only to her, but to others watching this display of flirtation climaxing before them on the night.

David smiled down at her. Standing at a good six foot three inches tall, he was an imposing sight. His dark beard and facial hair accentuated his light green, brown eyes. His smile widened in a way that made his eyes drill down into her soul.

"Sam?" he took his time to respond, teasing her with a wide grin. He licked his lips, now dry from the cold night air. "Sam… don't you think you would remember me if we had met before?" he flirted with her.

Samantha's stomach dropped. Her heart sunk with disappointment as she heard the answer to the question she had wanted to ask this stranger for the last three hours or more.

"I'm sorry. I just…" she stammered again. Words were deserting her. "It just… it feels like we have met before." She left the final comment in the air, hopeful that her declaration might trigger in him some repressed memory of a previous rendezvous.

"Sam, we have to catch up to the group again." He ushered her to the waiting crowd who were ready to begin their long-awaited tour of the Cemetery of the Capuchins. He seemed dismissive of her disclosure of closeness.

Her chest rose as she chose this moment to remind him again, "And I prefer Samantha, not Sam."

He smirked back at her without saying a word. Absolutely unfazed at the reminder.

"And I prefer Sam. That is the name I am always going to remember you by."

David's entrance to the much-loved tourist attraction was well received, having barely walked through the door before being sought after by a bevy of smiling Italian women, staff members of the church, obviously waiting eagerly to see him again.

"Buongiorno Bellissimo! Hello beautiful!" David greeted each of the women warmly with kisses to both cheeks, often having to reach over counters or bench tops to make contact with his affectionate friends.

Samantha and the green group watched on, as David was required to complete each and every welcome in person. Samantha's mind was reassured somewhat at watching the comfort he shared with each woman. His remark of calling her beautiful just a short time earlier seemed much less out of place to her now as he assigned the same endearing narrative to each friend he greeted. Samantha watched on as the women, eyes glued to David, flirted back with him. There was no denying this man had sex appeal. Not one female she had witnessed tonight had been immune to his obvious charm.

THREE

The Cemetery of the Capuchins, Rome, Italy

The tour continued and as Samantha stood in the fourth chapel of The Cemetery of the Capuchins, she was overwhelmed once more. This time by the thousands of bone fragments that decorated the walls, roof and corridor with thoughtful precision and calculation. The floor of the Chapel itself covered in dirt from Israel said to possess amazing powers of preservation. David told the story of a bouquet of flowers placed on the dirt remaining alive and preserved for weeks.

There was believed to be the remains of three thousand, seven hundred bodies in the tiny chapels located beneath the church. Thousands of bones adorned every available space before them; femurs, humeri, fibulas, scapulae and clavicles but mainly skulls. This was, after all nicknamed the skull chapel. They were told that current law prohibits human remains to be placed as displays of this kind, so if a single bone was to fall it must be afforded a proper burial. This would not be the first burial these remains had bared witness to but it would be their last.

At the centre of the impressive commemoration, two arms crossed in solidarity, said to represent both man and Christ and symbolise that they are one in the same. Both man - both vulnerable. The imagined faces of the hundreds of skulls staring back at the group spoke to each of the tourists. The impermanence of life, the certainty of death for each of the wide-eyed travellers in plain view for them all as a reminder of their own predetermined fate.

The room held the group in awe. Not only, of the hundreds of souls lost, but at the mastery of the artwork. The skulls once hidden behind the face of mortal man now lined neatly against the plastered wall of the ancient church. Row after row of the human skeletons placed with care to form intricate patterns in the decorative chapel. In the corners and at either side of the room, the garment of the Capuchin friars stood, arms folded in front. Their skulls holding in place the hood of the worn garment. Small crosses stood positioned in the ground below. The inscriptions of the sacred placements weathered by time. The small chapel was a transparent reminder of the swift passage of life and one's mortality.

The group ventured further down the corridor as David asked another question that few from the group seemed to be able to answer.

"What do you notice about this clock?"

The group was quiet until the attentive mother from London spoke, "It has no hands."

It seemed a strange answer given that the clock that sat majestically before them was made up entirely of finger bones and vertebrae.

The group stared at the clock on the wall. The indicators of time measuring to VI each formed with carefully placed finger bones nailed to the wall behind them. The outer rim of the circular piece was adorned by vertebrae, inside which more bones were placed to create an inner sphere.

David continued, "And what do you think is the meaning behind the clock?"

The visiting mother spoke again, obviously pleased to have made the connection, "It means time can't be controlled."

Samantha nodded her head in agreement. This message was becoming clearer and clearer as she made her way through Italy. Time flies. Time waits for no man. You can't turn back the hands of time. How many different ways did she need to hear the same message and yet what had she done for most of her life. She had wasted the most precious commodity she had been given - time.

David instructed the group to move to the final chapel.

"Come forward everyone. I want everyone to get a good look at this one. Come on, squash up. We are all friends here now. Sam, move a little closer up this way."

David placed his hand around Samantha and maneuvered her closer to him. The group was silent as David once more told of the history of the monks' remains displayed prominently before them.

"Now, do you remember what we said before about time?" he asked. The group hummed in agreement as if entranced by his words as they waited for him to continue.

"So, remember what the message here is. It's about time and this is what this final chapel represents to me. We bring you here not to feel any fear for what is displayed, not to feel any sadness for the people whose lives are now over. Instead, this journey tonight is about time and making sure we use our time wisely. Death is the ultimate leveller- none of us can control it and none of us can afford to waste the precious days we have been given to live our lives."

The group was thoughtful as they stood, some holding tightly the wrought iron black bars that separated themselves from the bones of the thousands of monks before them. Every one of the tour group was taking their individual time to absorb his words and the messages within them. Eyes darted from left to right, from the floor to the ceiling. Samantha herself tried to take in every inch of the scene before her, knowing one day it would just be her memory of this image alone that she would need to rely on.

Samantha felt David's presence close. He had barely moved more than a couple of feet from her for the entire time they had been in the narrow corridor that displayed the monks' remains. She felt the warmth of David's chest against her back. She felt once more his hand on her.

David pulled Samantha in closer. He leant down and whispered into her ear.

"Hanoi… The Temple of the Horse."

Samantha knew instantly what those words meant. That was how she recognised David. She had seen him in Vietnam, about a year or so earlier, inside The Temple of the Horse. The temple was a stunning little chapel located down a small alleyway in the Old Quarter of the dusty streets of Hanoi, Vietnam.

"That was you!" she smiled as the mystery unfolded.

"And that was you!" he smiled back.

Without taking a pause, he addressed the group again, "And that my good people, is the end of our tour tonight. I will give you a chance to have a look through the bookshop and I will be on the stairs outside to answer any final questions you might have. Take your time."

David looked down once more into Samantha's eyes, "See you outside beautiful," he toyed with her.

Samantha felt her body shake as she once again found a quiet place to still her mind. Hanoi. Of course, she thought to herself. She remembered the day well, she had thought about it often, the day she nearly met the dark haired stranger in The Temple of the Horse. In Vietnam it is custom for temples to have a theme or main point of interest and she just happened to walk into The Temple of the Horse one day while getting lost in the Old Quarter of Hanoi.

The temple was one that didn't allow photos, which meant Samantha stood in silence taking it all in. She walked into the main temple and found the most elegant statue of a grey horse she had ever seen. The horse had eyelashes; long eyelashes that made its eyes pop and gave them life. The horse brought back lovely memories of the father she had lost years earlier. In that moment she lowered her head in prayer to honour her beloved parent.

As she closed her eyes, she remembered the loving, caring man that was her father. She spoke to him, quietly telling him she loved him, when she was suddenly startled by someone closeby to her. She looked over and caught the eyes of a stranger staring back at her. Feeling slightly teary at the loss of the father she loved so much, she made her way to the door for some fresh air. Not that the air was in any way refreshing at that time of the year in Hanoi. The temperatures had been constantly hitting a high and humid thirty-six to thirty-eight degrees every day.

Sitting down on the front steps of the temple, she allowed a few light tears to flow. Once upon a time there would have been no stopping the tears from flowing freely at the memory of what she had lost, but over time she was able to control the sadness behind the grief to focus more and more on the loving memories that she carried in her heart of her beloved father.

She looked up again and the stranger was in front of her. She saw him walk toward her and then turn suddenly. She wondered if he was going to ask for directions and she tried her hardest to pull herself together. She realised she didn't look her most respectable at that present point in time. Sitting on a step in the dirt, shoes still removed as is respectful in the temple, tears rolling down her face, sniffling slightly, sweating profusely, she glanced up at the stranger. His amazing eyes bore down on her. He appeared to want to say something. She nearly spoke a word of greeting to him. He opened his mouth and then turned again.

Samantha looked down into her bag to find a tissue. She took a moment to gather herself before standing, ready to leave the temple grounds. She glanced around momentarily for the handsome stranger with the piercing eyes but he was gone.

Samantha had thought often about that day. It was obvious the stranger had wanted to say something. She didn't know what, and she regretted never finding out. And now, only twelve months later, here he was in Rome.

Samantha felt empowered. She headed to the bookstore after the tour, which was not something she wouldn't ever normally do. She purchased two postcards to remind her of the astounding images she had seen but had been unable to photograph due to the tight restrictions protecting the remains against photography.

She stood in line behind a young family from Dubai and watched as the father tried on bracelets. When it was her turn at the counter, she asked to see one of the bracelets, a series of small black skulls joined by a sturdy piece of black string. Yes, this was what she needed; a reminder, a constant reminder of how precious time was.

She made her purchase and headed outside into the cold night air to hear David's final words of wisdom for Rome. She couldn't wait and took the bracelet out of the packet and placed it on her left wrist. As she turned each skull over she saw the slight imperfections of each one. A large crack in the top of one, a deformed eye socket in another. Just amazing, she thought to herself, another reminder of the imperfect beauty of the human form.

"Sam?" David startled her from her daydream. "Are you ok?" His final speech was over.

"Yes, just lost in my thoughts," she reassured him.

"Did you enjoy the tour of the crypts and the catacombs?"

She stopped and thought before answering honestly, "Yes, it has given me a lot to think about."

"Sam... do you remember?" His words were quiet and hopeful. He was referring once more to their near meeting in Hanoi.

"Yes absolutely. I was a crying, dirty, sweaty mess on the step of the temple and you were going to speak to me."

"I wanted to but I saw that you were upset so I wanted to give you a couple of minutes and then I turned around and you were gone. I walked up and down the street looking for you. I had hoped to see you again in Vietnam. I looked out for you everywhere I went."

Samantha laughed and the more she laughed the harder she laughed. David joined her; the relief for him was immense. He was grateful that she remembered him as well.

"David, I searched everywhere I went for you as well. How insane is that?" She touched his face lightly. "You didn't have the beard back then. You looked very different."

"Vietnam was far too hot to wear this thing," he replied as he scratched his dark beard with his thumb and his forefinger. He was thoughtful for a moment as he stared directly into her hopeful eyes.

"Sam, this is the sanest thing that has ever happened to me." He reached down and cupped her chin. "I am going to kiss you now before you have a chance to run away again."

He lowered his head and placed his mouth on hers. Samantha reached around his waist and held him tightly. Nothing had felt more comfortable or more right to her in her entire life before. Their kiss was slow and heartfelt. His lips delicately skimmed over her sensitive skin. His tongue flirted with her lips before finding her welcoming mouth.

Samantha allowed every ounce of her being to relax and melt into the moment. Her body was limp but at the same time electric and alive. She relaxed and enjoyed the feeling of every single sensation.

"David? Excuse me?" The male American accent broke through their moment of passion.

David paused and sighed as he pulled his mouth away from Samantha's. "I won't be a moment. Don't go anywhere!" he warned her.

David walked toward the last remaining tour guest, obviously lost and feeling helpless in the massive city, he needed help with directions from his experienced guide.

Samantha felt for the cold stone pillar behind her for support. She traced her bottom lip with her tongue to taste David once more. She felt alive but so very calm. She had once read that when you meet your soulmate, there wouldn't be fireworks or instant passion and lust but instead an intense feeling of calm and peace.

"Soulmate," she laughed to herself. There she was getting ahead of herself again. It was one kiss. Just one kiss she had to remind herself.

David returned to her side, "Let's get out of here."

Without waiting for a response, he once again took Samantha's hand and walked her down the stairs of the magnificent church. He stopped halfway, turned to her and kissed her once more. This time the passion and lust were undeniable. His breath was warm and his mouth sweet. Samantha could feel her new bracelet on her wrist. The small black skulls reminding her that time is short.

"David," she stopped him, "I am renting a loft just a street away. Will you come back with me?"

He looked down at her and smiled. "I thought you would never ask," he teased her.

Neither of the two will ever remember the few moments it took to walk to the loft. Instead both anticipating what was to come, they walked quickly and with purpose. They strode to the loft in a dream-like state, both grinning, both silent as their minds raced with endless possibilities.

They climbed the narrow spiral staircase to the small quiet loft in the centre of Rome. The room was hot from the timed heating that was working it's magic, so Samantha opened the door to the small terrace for two. The cool breeze through the door was a relief as the heat of their bodies once more joined and grew exponentially.

They removed their jackets, which were soon discarded on the floor. Samantha wasted no time and began to tug at David's jumper. He released it without a fight. He pulled Samantha's scarf above her head and began unbuttoning her jeans. She skilfully kicked off her boots and worked quickly on removing his t-shirt before starting on the zipper of his pants.

Clothes were falling to the ground, layers upon layers of unraveling, like a delicious, decadent desert. David stopped.

"Sam, are you sure this is what you want?"

Samantha lifted her left wrist to display the symbol of time to him. "I am not wasting a mere second more thinking about how much I want this."

With that, David lifted her legs around his waist and carried her to the bed. With just a thin layer of material separating them, he removed the last shred of her clothing to stand for a moment and take in the beauty of the woman before him. He licked his lips again. He removed his final piece of clothing and lay down next to Samantha. For a moment, she was fearful that he didn't want to continue.

"What is it?" she begged of him.

"I just can't believe this is happening. That you are here."

She imagined she could almost see tears well in his eyes.

"David… make love to me." Her words were pleading, lustful and without patience.

David rolled toward her and immediately joined with her. There was no time to waste. They needed to feel their bodies join. They craved to feel as close as two people could feel.

* * *

Samantha woke in his arms. The cold air from the open terrace door stirred through the room but couldn't penetrate the warm and protective capsule they had formed together. She rolled over to face him and stared at her sleeping David. He stirred ever so slightly and she kissed his lips. His eyes fluttered open and his immediate smile shined through the darkened room.

"I didn't just dream it then?" he asked her.

She kissed him again.

"Shh… go back to sleep now." She snuggled into his chest and closed her eyes. She couldn't ever remember a time she felt so right about anything before. She planted one final kiss on his bare chest and fell into a peaceful slumber.

FOUR

Rome, Italy

Samantha woke early the following morning. The sun hadn't risen in Rome. She heard soft raindrops, which seemed commonplace in the early mornings for the time of year. She quietly stepped over to the small kitchenette and made herself an espresso. Once done, she took one final look at the sleeping David before she walked through the open door and out onto the small terrace.

Her body was tingling from the warm kisses on her skin from the night before. She had never felt so alive. She smiled to herself and closed her eyes to relive the dream that was the last few hours of her life. Being philosophical by nature, she smirked at how a life can be changed in just a few short hours. People can come into your life. People can leave. Death can come that quickly and it could all be over. But most of all, she smiled in the knowledge that whatever happened in her future, her life had changed undeniably within just a few precious hours. She knew nothing would ever be the same for her again.

David woke and for a moment feared he had lost her once more. Her scent, left on the pillow of the empty bed, the telling sign that she wasn't too far away. He slowly made his way to the edge of the bed, sitting upright his feet found the solid floor. He felt groggy. He was normally a quick to rise, jump out of bed to start the day kind of guy, but on that morning his actions were stalled and slow.

He made his way to follow the aroma of the freshly brewed coffee and was pleased to find enough for two. He poured a small cup and walked to the terrace door. He made it to the exit just as she turned to smile at him. She looked radiant sitting under the transparent awning, huddled under a thick blanket covering herself from the cold and the rain. Against the dark and gloomy winter sky, her face shone like an angel.

He didn't know what to say or do. It all felt like a dream to him. How he ever got so lucky as to find her once more, he couldn't imagine. But to find her in the wide world not just once or twice but three times was beyond belief. This was a sign to him that they were meant to be together and whatever was to happen next, he was determined to do whatever he could to not lose the woman he loved again.

He stepped out onto the terrace, "So, Samantha from Australia… what do we do now?"

She smiled as she teased him, "Wow, David from California, we have only just met. Enough with the pressure to commit already."

He laughed at her coyness but feared what might secretly be behind her words.

"Technically, we haven't… just… met. We have met before, you do remember?"

She was quick to correct him, "Well actually we didn't really technically meet in Vietnam. Sure, we saw each other and acknowledged each other but we didn't officially introduce ourselves, now did we?"

David's concern was peaked. He realised that Samantha hadn't fully recognised him yet. Sure, she remembered the exchange in Hanoi but she hadn't seemed to piece the puzzle together completely. She didn't seem to remember their first real meeting. David was being placed in a difficult situation. The realisation of who they actually were to each other needed to be articulated. He wasn't sure if she would even believe him if he confessed the truth to her. She was his Samantha from Australia. She just didn't realise it yet.

Given her failure to recall their first chance meeting, David was left wondering if maybe she wasn't the Samantha he remembered from all those years ago. He stopped his mind from racing and stared at the gorgeous woman in front of him. He quickly put any doubt out of his mind. He knew this was his Samantha. He just wondered how long it would take for her to remember and truly recognise him as well.

David was keen to confirm the practicalities of their new situation. "How long are you in Rome for?" he asked.

Samantha took a gulp of her coffee to delay her response. She wasn't sure David was going to like her answer.

"I leave tomorrow for Florence."

She looked up at him and waited for his response. It was quick to come, as if any prolonged or agonised thought played no part in what was to happen next for the happy couple.

"Would you like company?" he smiled back at her. He was not prepared to even entertain the thought of letting her go already. It was an instant decision to join her in Florence. To extend the current adventure for as long as he could was the only possible decision he could make.

She placed her cup down with a heavy thud and jumped from the seat. The blanket fell to the ground as she embraced David tightly with both arms.

"I would love you to come!" she shouted with excitement. It was as if every romantic fantasy she had ever had of travelling through Europe was coming true.

David quickly realised the opportunity of his situation. If his brain hadn't immediately registered it for him, his penis surely did. As Samantha now embraced him, untethered from the large blanket, she stood before him completely naked. With his spare hand, he reached down and playfully cupped her firm bottom, making her conscious, for the first time of the vulnerability of her nakedness and the absence of her clothing.

"You would love me to do what now?" he teased her with a sexy whisper.

Samantha was quick to register the intent behind the sexy murmurings, "I said… I would love you to come."

David reached his long arm around her waist and lifted her gently over the step of the terrace door. She squealed with delight. She pushed the door closed as she moved into the room, and reached out and took David's coffee from his hand. She took a quick swig of the hot brew and placed it effortlessly on the small table as she was carried through the room.

David threw her onto the bed, standing sternly above her looking down at her once more. His manhood at full erection ready for the foreplay he craved.

"Say it once more for me Sam."

Samantha giggled like a nervous teenager. She grabbed the pillow and placed it across her body to cover her nakedness. She was excited about what was to happen and very aware of the vulnerability her exposure stirred in her.

David placed his hands on his hips, which did nothing to hide his rising erection. She wondered if he was purposefully drawing her eyes to it. Not that she could miss it.

"Sam… I won't ask you again. Now tell me what you would like for me to do?"

Samantha giggled. "I would like you to come to Florence with me!" The excitement of her saying it out loud again made her scream with pure joy.

"That's my Sam."

David seemed pleased with the obedience of his more than willing partner. He hurled himself onto the bed and grabbed the pillow from Samantha to expose her nakedness, before kissing every inch of her body.

Samantha closed her eyes and breathed in the scent of this gorgeous man. Her body now cold from the exposure to the morning air exploded with pure ecstasy every time his warm mouth touched her skin.

She smiled a smile so involuntary that she couldn't stop it if she had wanted to. Samantha was the happiest she had ever been. There were no questions, no doubts, no answers that needed to be found. She was one hundred percent purely content.

Rome had been good for Samantha's soul in more ways than one. The food, the sounds, the history and the people all made her come alive. Rome just had that effect on a person. There is no need to rush anywhere, after all history dictated that the city had been around for a very, very, long time, over 2770 years to be exact, or possibly not so exact. One person's small amount of rushing really wasn't going to have any consequence at all. And the beautiful people of Rome took the time to say Buongiorno. They forced their visitors to slow down and enjoy every beauty the ancient city had to offer them.

Her European trip was working perfectly. It was having the exact effect it was meant to have on her soul. Her time in Rome had been short but it felt to Samantha as if she had been away for months already. To her this was yet another example of the preciousness of time.

There were two main thoughts running through Samantha's head as she packed her bag the next morning for Florence - time and penises. The philosophical ponderings of time, well she had started to process and act on that one a little already. The thoughts about penises, well that had been a surprising new twist to her adventures, but one she was more than happy to continue to explore.

There were many reasons for the thoughts of the male appendage besides David of course. And that was probably because there were reminders everywhere in Rome, and maybe also because Samantha had just completed a trip to the archeological site of Pompeii and the male form featured extensively there as well.

It was beyond belief to think that under twenty feet of volcanic ash and pumice that spewed from Mount Vesuvius there lay dormant for 1500 thousand years were so many artwork penises. They were on the fronts of building, they were etched into the stonework on the roadways, and they were in paintings, sculptures, and advertisements for leisurely pursuits. The symbol of the male erection was even on the menu for brothels displaying the various positions on offer in each establishment.

Pompeii had been on Samantha's bucket list for as long as she could remember. She was moved by the fossilised human remains. She was touched by the orange tree that grew strong and tall in the middle of what was once charred and ashen ground. Most of all, she was taken back to a time when life seemed more simple. Community was smaller, neighbours knew each other and every working efficiency of town planning just seemed more sensible.

The cobbled paths of Pompeii allowed for the rain to wash away the excrement of the animals used to move stock and people from one place to the next. The furniture, made of stone was indestructible even to the immense heat of the volcanic spill. She could almost imagine the life that flowed through the streets of the small city. The amount of penis signs, statues and symbols alluded to a people who knew that joy was often found in the simple pleasures of life.

The symbol was of course, also the sign of good luck and fertility. And there was nothing wrong with that as far as Samantha was concerned. Of course, lots of good things come from the male genitalia, two that sprung to mind for Samantha were orgasms and children. Both of which many people have enjoyed time and time again. So, if the penis was to be the national symbol of hope and good fortune, so be it, she wasn't going to complain.

Of course, Samantha was a hopeless romantic and for her the penis also symbolised a man in love. She wasn't about to argue with the Italians the difference between love and lust, she was just happy, for the time being to admit they both had their merits.

Samantha recalled one of her favourite artworks found in the ashes of Pompeii. One of the few she had seen that hadn't represented the male form in some way. A mosaic piece illustrating the certainty and finality of death. The symbol of death balancing a set of scales. Weighing down the end of each scale was an item of clothing. On one side, a worn and tattered piece of cloth representing a dress barely held together after years of wear. The owner of an item such as this, certainly unable to replace it. The unfortunate circumstances of poverty ensuring such financial hardship. On the other side of the scale, a bejeweled red gown symbolising wealth and prosperity. The owner of an item like this, likely enjoying a full and luxurious wardrobe.

Samantha remembered photographing the piece, trying to capture the essence of the meaning behind the impressive artwork. Death the ultimate leveller, determining the end of one's life. No wealth or standing in community being able to ward off the grim reaper when he came to visit. The poor and impoverished standing alongside the well-to-do, facing death directly, no favour granted to either for the circumstances of their life when death came to take them away.

As she shook her head, Samantha thought back momentarily to the death that had so far surrounded her. If only, she wondered, if only she had time to do over again, would she do it differently? Would there be more words that needed to be spoken? More affection to be shown? Would there be more places she would take her loved ones before they left her for good? What she wouldn't give for just one more day with her much loved family members.

She wondered what they would think of her travel to Rome and what they would make of the gorgeous David. Would they encourage her to run off to Florence with the handsome stranger or would they encourage her to take her time and to guard her heart?

Would they ask her to remember that not everyone's intentions are as pure and loving as her own?

Samantha smiled as she remembered a brief encounter of pure intentions that would be one of the pleasant highlights from her trip. A lovely and very professional taxi driver who had taken her on a little side trip of Rome before he dropped her off at her destination.

"Look to the right, do you see the centurion guard?" the driver asked Samantha.

"Yes, yes. He is dressed in traditional ancient uniform."

He went on to explain that every day a guard was to stand watch over the government building. He stands there for his entire shift. His weapon held upright on the ground beside him.

"We mustn't stop long. Someone will be out to chase us away," the driver warned.

As he dropped her off at her final destination, he waited for her to exit the cab and nearly close the door before he said to her, "And now, I get to tell you how beautiful you are!" he smiled as he spoke.

"Grazie," was her reply to acknowledge his very kind compliment.

"I couldn't tell you in the taxi, so I tell you now, I have to tell you, how very, very beautiful you are."

Samantha almost cried. No one had said that to her in a very long time. It took a stranger in a foreign country to make her feel just that little special again. The empowered woman in her wanted to roar, to remind herself that she didn't need external influences to feel special but she shut her down to just enjoy the moment of connection with this stranger who wanted nothing more than to express his appreciation of a thing of beauty.

As her time in Rome was about to end, Samantha was grateful for her wonderful memories of the beautiful ancient city. Amongst all of those memories, the ones that made Samantha smile the most were the reminders of time and penises. Why she kept thinking of penis in the plural she didn't know, because she only really needed the one. The buzzer sounded as if on cue and David's voice echoed through the intercom phone.

"Are you ready, beautiful?"

"I'll come straight down," Samantha replied.

She was a little sad to be leaving Rome but overjoyed at the idea of travelling through Florence with the gorgeous David. She still couldn't believe her luck. How was it possible that they found each other again? So often she had thought of that day in Hanoi and the lost opportunity when she failed to talk to the handsome bright-eyed stranger from the temple. But all was not lost and sometimes, some things are just meant to be. Life seems to find a way to make things happen just the way they should do.

The train ride to Florence was romantic. Samantha cuddled into David. They kissed. They looked into each other's eyes. They were the type of couple that normally made Samantha scoff at such public displays of affection. She had become one of those people. But for once she didn't care what anyone else thought. She was living the stuff of romantic novels and she didn't care about anything else. She was determined to enjoy her time to be spontaneous, romantic and impulsive.

David couldn't have felt more different. David had never imagined he could be so lucky as to find her again that his head was circled with questions, possibilities and scenarios on how he could ensure he didn't let this woman he loved slip through his hands one more time.

He still hadn't worked out how he might trigger Samantha's earliest memory of them. The obvious answer was to tell her outright, but where was the fun in that? He also seriously questioned her believing it considering the incredible nature of the story.

David had of course visited Florence before, being the world traveller he was. And given that he took his role of tour guide very seriously, he had wanted to learn as much as he could about Italian history, not just confining it to Rome. He looked forward to playing the role of personal tour guide to Samantha and had planned some very special surprises for her. Starting of course with the stunning apartment he had rented. Wide windows stared out at the Piazza Signorini. With the windows open the whole square came into view and the sights and sounds entered their space and overtook the senses with music, laughter and beauty.

"See that tower over there?" David pointed to the clock tower sitting majestically over the square dominating it with its rich but dark history. "Tomorrow we are going to climb that!" he informed her excitedly. "I hope you're not scared of heights," he added.

"I'm not scared of anything anymore," she replied.

"Two hundred and twenty-three stone stairs to the top will take us to the highest battlemented level." David was excited about sharing this special experience with Samantha. "The view from the top is magnificent." David paused before adding, "And if you are lucky, I might even take you into the excavations of the Roman Theatre of Florence beneath the Palazzo Vecchio. It's a little dark and eerie down there. I hope you can handle it."

"I also want to go and see Michelangelo's David," Samantha added.

David turned to face her, arms outstretched, his wide smile flashed across his face. "You're seeing it right now beautiful!" he laughed at his own corniness.

"Really?" Samantha felt flirty. She couldn't resist the stunning creature in front of her. He was right. She had got lucky and scored herself her very own David in Florence.

"Um, the other David is naked," she didn't hesitate to point out.

Without delay his clothes were off and David assumed the pose of Michelangelo's famous statue, right there in their little apartment. The chill from the windows didn't have the very unfortunate effect it could have and he stood there for her posing in all his magnificent glory.

Samantha couldn't help but stare and this time it wasn't at his eyes. "You do have the most glorious penis." Her sexy hushed tone leaving little question as to the thought racing into her mind.

That was all the encouragement he needed. David once more joined Samantha as she giggled with pleasure.

FIVE

Firenze, Italy

The Museo di Palazzo Vecchio didn't fail to disappoint as David guided Samantha through each level of the elegant building. The first floor housed the Salone dei Cinquecento or Hall of the Five Hundred, said to be the most impressive room of the building still the city's primary venue for ceremonial events. Taking in every inch of its beauty, David enticed her into the room of secret doors and shared with her the building's mystery and cleverly designed network of passageways and connecting rooms.

She felt his hand grip hers as with the other he pointed out and described in detail one priceless artwork after another and yet another. Samantha hadn't seen anything more beautiful, made even more memorable by the close contact and special one-on-one guided tour she enjoyed.

Taking to the narrow stone stairwell leading to the battlement, the duo hiked the ninety-five metres to the top of the Tower of Palazzo Vecchio. The stairs were a simple ascent, their spacing well designed and little effort was required to reach the top, but once there Samantha's persistent cough started up again. Once more David reached into his pocket to hand her a Halls lozenge.

"Do you think you should see a doctor about that?" he asked with genuine concern.

"No, it's fine. It is just annoying. It doesn't hurt at all."

A visit to a doctor or hospital was the last thing on Samantha's mind. She had a very real aversion to medical attention and avoided visits to the doctor at all costs. She knew it wasn't at all a healthy avoidance but she couldn't stand the sights, smells and feel of medical offices.

She turned her attention to the view which unfolded in front of them. As they stepped onto the wooden platform to gain the best vantage point they stood silent as they embraced the centuries of beauty before them. David reached for Samantha's hand once more.

"Sam…" David began. He was hesitant. He didn't know what or how to say what he needed to say to Samantha.

Samantha turned to face him. She viewed what she perceived to be a look of anguish on his gorgeous face.

"What is it?" She needed him to say what was on his mind.

He turned to face her, bringing her closer to him as he spoke. "I don't want to lose you ever again," he admitted to her.

She smiled at him. Her relief at the admission was flattering and mirrored her very own thoughts. The extent of which not yet ready to be expressed openly.

"You won't lose me," she promised him.

He smiled as he kissed her mouth gently.

As they took in the breathtaking view, the cool breeze caused her to cough once more. She covered her mouth and let out a dry, hoarse cough. David hugged her tightly.

"Let's get you home to bed before you get sick up here in the cold wind."

"Seriously, is that all you ever think about?" she flirted shamelessly with him.

"With you around it is hard to think of anything else," he assured her.

Before making their way to the apartment above the square, Samantha was able to convince David to indulge her some more and take in the tour of the archaeological excavations of the Roman Theatre of Florence. As David had promised, the site did not disappoint. The use of clever imagery using human form, music and movement made the ruins come alive. The dark surrounds gave way to the colourful dancing children, the boy carrying a flame and finally the mother and child before the images, like the people they represented disappeared once more into the blackness of the desolated buildings around them.

They found themselves alone amongst the ruins. The noise from the levels of tourists above quietened as they walked further and further into the underground remains. They were silent, looking around, walking gently as to pay respect for the formations that once stood in that very spot. An eerie but warm atmosphere penetrated them both. They held hands as they stopped once more for a gentle and loving kiss.

There was something spiritual about the ruins. Maybe it was the energy of all those who had called the site their home. Maybe it was the careful and meticulous way the area had been excavated and restored, allowing the ancient building works to be uncovered. Each brick in the carefully built formations were placed there by the hand of a person, long passed. Samantha reached out and stroked the nearest brick. Its hard surface was cold to the touch. She tried to etch every piece of the excavation site into her long-term memory. She didn't want to ever forget a moment of this magical day.

When finally they arrived back to their cosy little apartment for two, they relaxed with a wine before beginning plans for their next big adventure.

"So, where to next?" he asked her.

"Well to see Michelangelo's David of course," she was quick to inform him.

"I keep telling you…" He paused before assuming the pose once more, "You have the real thing right here."

The two laughed and drunk more wine, finding music in the rented apartment they danced and chatted for hours. The night ended with the lovers in each other's arms once more. They slept soundly as if this was the place their bodies needed to be, entwined in each other, naked and exposed, requiring only each other for their ongoing existence in the world.

The following day as promised David took Samantha to visit the famous Galleria dell Accademia housing the world-renowned statue of Michelangelo's David in all his alabaster glory. Samantha's David was more than happy to play photographer for the pair, taking the required photos of Samantha in front of the statue. Samantha took charge of the camera for a quick sneak peek at what she had heard was his equally magnificently-formed bottom.

The pair giggled like young children as they explored one room after another of the museum's most rare and valued pieces. The beauty that this one building held was beyond description. Samantha paused as one particular statue caught her attention. It was the statue entitled Love, Vice and Wisdom or The Sleep of Ill-fated Virtue and of Lustful Opulence, The Disc of Loves, The World. Much as the title described, the statue represented an allegory of the world, symbolised by the circulatory nature of the disc, which formed the platform of the piece. Three children formed the centre of the piece; the first being Virtue, a child asleep being crushed by the child, Vice who laid down as a bowl slips from his hands. The third child, in the middle of the disc, pointing upward to represent Love, as the force that dominates the world.

Samantha was quite taken by the piece and photographed it from every possible angle in an attempt to capture its complexity and wisdom. David watched on from the far end of the room. His arms folded as he witnessed his lover do what she enjoyed best. He was immensely relieved that he had found her and that Samantha had embraced their new relationship with the same enthusiasm and lack of trepidation that he himself had felt.

He still couldn't believe this had happened. The girl with whom he shared his first kiss, the girl he had remembered in his heart forever, had arrived in his new home, in the city of Rome and walked directly back into his life. He didn't need any clearer sign that this woman was to share his life with him. He felt overjoyed but also amazingly calm and confident that everything he had ever wanted had just become a reality.

He smiled as he watched Samantha work her magic with the camera. She looked up between shots, and searched the room for him. Their eyes made contact and they connected once more. No words needed. They both understood through a look that they were there for each other and needed no further reassurance.

David understood exactly what had captured Samantha's attention with the statue. It was one of his favourite features as well. The symbolism of the universe and particularly one with the use of small children as the markers of human desire and ego conveyed a strong message. He couldn't break his stare. He was enthralled as he watched his lover enact one of her great passions, taking photo after photo of the art piece.

Once finished, Samantha walked over to join David as they made their way to the exit of the museum. Walking past the statue of David a final time, they both stopped to take in its magnificence once more. Samantha giggled at the wicked thought that entered her head. David knowing exactly what she was thinking leaned in to chastise her. "You have a dirty mind." Although attempting to be serious with her, David was secretly very pleased that Samantha was an intensely sexual being.

Samantha leaned in to whisper to him, "Your penis is much nicer," she flirted with him.

"Nicer?" He tilted his head and raised his left brow to question her underwhelming choice of word.

"Glorious then?" Samantha flirted back, "Is that a more fitting description for it?"

"That's a little better."

He wrapped his strong arm around her and leaned down to kiss her soft lips. Her cheeks slightly flushed from the verbal foreplay, did little to hide her intent.

"Should we head back to the apartment then?" David suggested.

"I think that would be an appropriate idea," Samantha agreed with him.

Making their way down the small alley that housed the Galleria dell Accademia, Samantha began to formulate her next blog post. Travel blogging was a new avenue she had begun to experiment with but unfortunately, she couldn't quite grasp the same enthusiasm for the blogging as she had for the travel itself.

Following an evening of passion, Samantha forced herself to crawl out from under the duvet in the early hours of the morning to find her laptop and press the key that forced it into life. She glanced at David, sleeping like a baby and was hopeful she wouldn't wake him. She began her first draft.

* * *

Blog Post - Rome

I lost my heart in Rome…
Travelling through Italy has been the most beautiful experience and I choose that word purposefully. Everything in Rome is beautiful; everyone I have met in this ancient city is beautiful. And it is the people most of all that contribute to this beauty. Unlike, traditional western cultures, the Italians and particularly the Romans have no interest in what you do for work. They appear to care little about how busy your career is or how you meet your key performance indicators for the month. This is a sweeping generalisation of course and I am sure there would be those in business in Rome that would enjoy eliciting those conversations with you, but for those working and living in the ancient district of Rome, those working with the tourism machine that perpetuates the hive of activity in the city, those individuals want to know about you, the person. It is a great

relief to not be asked immediately, what you do for work, but instead asked about who your family is, where you are from and what you love. These seem to be the central three questions afforded to a new acquaintance in Rome and once these parameters or criteria are addressed, a new friendship is formed. It really appears to be that easy.

It seems to me similar to primary or nursery school where friendships are formed instantly based on mutual love. Two young girls enjoy the same music and they are bonded. Young boys, bond on the football field and become lifelong friends. The complexity of modern society is forgotten or rejected, whichever may be the case in this city of beauty. And once those parameters are determined and the friendship is formed, the two new acquaintances go about the business of enjoying the beauty together.

And for those of you with an idea of what that means, yes, this beauty can absolutely be found in the desire of the flesh but this is one and only one avenue for the exploration of beauty. Beauty is found in every corner of this impressive city. It is found in every narrow alley and in every cobblestoned piazza. Beauty is present in every movement, sound, touch and feel that tantalises the senses. Your new Roman friend will seek out with you, beautiful food, music, wine or as the locals prefer, Limoncello, the Italian made lemon liquor they will so fondly serve you and insist you enjoy. In some cases, the enjoyment of Limoncello is a long and entertaining process that can last many hours, long into the night as if each new tasting will be miraculously different to the last.

It would appear to this wide-eyed traveller that exploring beauty in Rome is the city's most treasured pastime. Well-known musicians take to the streets to play for the crowds, asking nothing but the purity of enjoyment and appreciation of the romantic sounds being created. Dining out is a gastronomic feast with every pasta and pizza imaginable being offered up as fare for the hungry tourist and local alike. The most passionate of the foodies offering just a little chilli or just a little special garlic sauce, fresh parmesan or locally made pure virgin olive oil to tantalise the senses even further. There is no point in declining the helpful suggestions; these artists know just what to add to turn the meal from food into an explosion of the taste buds.

Artwork, statues and ornate facades of buildings burst from every pore of the mighty ancient city. Influences from Egypt, massive pillars and obelisks create a sense of majesty and greatness. The beauty of the city itself challenges the traveller and dares one not to fall in love. The archeological lasagna as it is called is the result of centuries of building a city torn down time and time again by the ravages of war and years. The hidden treasures beneath old churches and museums, incomprehensible from the outside, supply miles of ancient ruins that will take your breath away. The imaginations of city life centuries before, forces the witness to testify to the rich history of this glorious city.

Beauty is not forced but adored in this busy place. A city never too rushed to stop and appreciate its uniqueness. For a traveller, a willing participant on the search, you will see, taste, hear, touch and feel beauty in every form. You will be appreciated yourself for the beauty of your soul. A lovely and very professional taxi driver showed me some of the local highlights, including a real-life centurion as he toured me across Rome one night. He waited until I had stepped from the vehicle to tell me I was beautiful. "I had to wait until you were out of the taxi to tell you how beautiful you are. You are very, very beautiful." He had obviously not wanted me to feel uncomfortable or threatened in any way. I swear the tears welled in my eyes. The strong, independent woman in me wanted to roar to herself for needing to have a complete stranger make her feel beautiful again. But this man, this Roman-born taxi driver wanted to appreciate and announce the beauty he saw. I could feel nothing but honoured by his compliment.

I will travel through Europe, meeting beautiful people and visiting beautiful places but for the challenge to seek beauty in everything I will never find anywhere like Rome.

A little bit of me, of my interaction with people will hopefully stay with those I meet along my journey, but forever and always a little bit of my heart will have been lost to Rome.

* * *

Samantha read over the piece one last time, hit the save draft button, closed the screen and looked around the room. It was strange how life had changed for her in such a short time. It was only a matter of weeks since the taxi driver told her she was beautiful and she was quite surprised at her reaction. And then, she found David who told her constantly how beautiful she was and how much he didn't want to lose her. There was no way she could ever have guessed she could get so lucky.

Just then the ringing of David's phone broke through the silence of the quiet night in Florence. He reached out as he barely managed to open one eye to grab for the now lit screen.

"Hello," David answered.

Samantha looked on wondering who would be ringing at that time of the morning. Glancing at the clock, it was barely three in the morning. She watched on as David took in the words of the caller. He sat upright, obviously now awake and appearing slightly unnerved by what he was hearing.

"When did this all happen?" he asked. Silently he listened for the answer. "I'll come straight away." There was a small pause as David looked up to meet Samantha's concerned eyes. "No, of course I can't stay away. I will catch the first flight. Tell her I love her and I am on my way." David hung up the phone and bowed his head.

"Is everything ok?" Samantha asked him.

David looked up. His face was the colour of the white sheet he sat beneath.

"It's my mother. She's had a bad accident…" He paused and collected his next thought. "You do understand, don't you? I have to go."

Samantha didn't hesitate. She couldn't imagine David would want to be anywhere else but beside his mother at this point in time.

"Of course I understand. Is she going to be ok?" Samantha hesitantly questioned him.

"They don't know… I hope so," David replied reluctantly.

SIX

California, United States

The plane trip back to California was agonisingly slow for David. All he wanted was to be home already and to find out the latest update on his mother's recovery. The timing of all of it couldn't have been worse. He was reluctant to leave Samantha behind but didn't want to impose on her to join him. He didn't want to let Samantha out of his sight, not yet anyway. Not after taking so long to find her again, but he needed to be home and with his family.

He raced off the plane as soon as he could get through the dawdling passengers. After the immigration check, he began a slow-paced jog to the entry gates and through the terminal. He made his way quickly past the masses of people in the busy airport to the exit. He needed not to waste time at the luggage carousel for he had just his cabin luggage, his well-travelled duffle bag. As David reached his destination in the fresh air past the airport door he searched for his brother's car.

The sound of the horn alerted David to its presence and he ran over to the white sedan, wasting no time in throwing his bag onto the back seat as he did. He greeted his brother with a long hug.

"Caleb, how is she?" he quickly asked, frantic for an update since he had boarded the plane hours earlier.

"She is not out of the woods yet. They are worried about swelling to the brain as a result of the fall. She hit her head pretty hard," Caleb informed his brother.

"What was she doing anyway?"

"She was trying to paint the corner of the ceiling. She used a small ladder to reach but she must have lost her balance and hit the floor with force," Caleb's voice trailed off as he spoke.

"But why didn't she just ask Dad to do it?" David was ravenous for more detail.

"You know what she is like, one stubborn old woman. She wanted it done immediately and couldn't wait for Dad to come home from golf."

David then spoke, more softly this time, "How's Dad?"

Caleb shook his head in response. "He's not good. Obviously blaming himself for not being there. He hasn't left her side."

The rest of the ride was taken up with further questions from David, some of which not even Caleb had the answers to. Both brothers were worried about their mother who had failed to gain consciousness since she was found unresponsive on the kitchen floor of their large family home. Their concern compounded by the fact that their father was unable to forgive himself of the guilt that had consumed him.

When they arrived at the hospital, Caleb showed his brother to the room and faded into the background to allow David to embrace their father. The two men stood and held each other tightly. David allowed his father's tears to fall as he stood strong holding the weight of his beloved parent as the older man literally fell into his son's arms.

"I can't believe she would do something so stupid." His father paused. "I would have done it for her, if only she would have waited."

The pain for David seeing his father in such extreme agony was unbearable.

"Dad, why don't you go home and get some sleep? I will stay with Mum. Caleb can drive you."

"That's ridiculous!" his father shouted back. "I'm not leaving her!"

David stood down immediately as he understood completely. If this was his Samantha, there would be no circumstance in which he could think of leaving her side. The small family took their place beside the bed of their much-cherished mother and wife.

The following morning, the doctor made his daily rounds and didn't have positive news for the family. The longer the patient was unconscious for, the less confidence they had of a full recovery from any permanent damage to brain function. They had hoped she would have woken by now but she so far had been unable to. The second and more concerning factor was that the swelling of the brain hadn't been as quick to respond to treatment as they had hoped, further complicating the chances of a speedy recovery.

The three men listened on, eager for some good news. They thanked the doctor for his patience in answering all of their questions and continued their bedside vigil. David examined the machine that breathed for his mother. He watched her chest rise and fall almost in rhythm to the sounds of the hospital equipment around him.

He watched his father, barely holding it together, occasionally closing his eyes to get the much-needed sleep he had deprived himself of for days now. Each time his eyelids closed and his head bowed, he caught himself dozing and sprung his head back up to wake himself.

David looked toward his younger brother. He was thankful that he had been back in their hometown at the time of the accident. With the amount of travel Caleb did for his online startup company, it was rare for him to be at home for any lengthy periods of time. Having Caleb nearby as everything unfolded must have been a huge relief to their father.

Each day had begun to blend into the next. The patient hadn't made the progress the doctors had hoped for and questions were beginning to be asked about the possibility of a recovery at all. David, Caleb and their father were being faced with some difficult conversations.

David had thought often of contacting Samantha but didn't want to take his focus from the people in the room that needed him the most. He had also wanted to be able to contact her with some positive news. He didn't want her to worry about him so decided to hold off messaging for a while longer. He hoped she would understand.

* * *

Samantha had made her own journey from Florence to Venice and was finding her way around the beautiful water-encased city with ease. She tried desperately to distract herself from her thoughts of David and his family. She had tried to contact him but had so far failed to receive a response in return. She hoped that didn't mean the worst had happened, but couldn't help but worry about the condition of his mother and the fact that David himself hadn't let her know how his mother was recovering.

Samantha couldn't help but be reminded of the long hours in hospital rooms she had spent with family who were unwell. A hospital room could conjure up such magical memories, as in the birth of a child. They also had the disarming ability to recall tragic memories and images of pure anguish and agony. Unfortunately for Samantha and never really fully knowing why, she had hated hospitals for as long as she remembered. She didn't quite know where her dislike of hospitals from a young child stemmed from. She did know that if David rang her and asked for her to be with him, she wouldn't hesitate. She highly doubted he would ask that of her given the current lack of contact from him at all.

Trying to focus on new experiences, Samantha enjoyed the best pasta meal she had eaten in Italy. The restaurant owner welcomed her as he seated her near the window so she could watch the crowds meander by. As she outlined her latest blog in her head, she caught out of the corner of her eye an overstated hand gesture. Her attention was required by a smiling waiter from the small bistro across the lane. He stood in the doorway of his establishment, blowing kisses to Samantha through the window. Samantha smiled and gave a small wave of acknowledgement back. She giggled a little at the hubris of the Italian man.

Days rolled around and Samantha was growing more and more concerned by David's lengthy absence and lack of reply to any of her attempts at communication with him. She had hoped she would have heard from him by now, even if it was to just to let her know he was ok.

She prayed that David's mother might have been well on the road to recovery by now. Samantha had an alarming thought come to mind. *What if she hadn't recovered? What if she…?* Samantha took a large gulp to prevent herself from finishing her final thought. Poor David, his poor family, she couldn't even imagine what could be happening for them at this moment.

Determined to get some final shots in before Samantha had to leave Venice, she grabbed her backpack and headed for the door once more. She made her way to the crowded Piazza San Marco. The square was home to the magnificent Basilica di San Marco, Venice's signature church first built to house the body of St Mark. It was a lavish building and the centrepiece of the busy tourist area of San Marco. Samantha tried in vain to get a photo of the impressive structure that didn't contain a pigeon in it. The square was known to be the home for tourists, pigeons and pickpockets. Samantha took a step back to again re-focus her camera.

"Oops sorry!" the male voice apologised to her as she squashed his foot beneath hers.

"Sorry. It was my fault I wasn't looking," she explained.

"No, my fault too. I wasn't paying attention. I had my eye glued to the camera," the man reassured her.

As Samantha composed herself, she took notice for the first time of this handsome stranger in front of her.

"Hi, I'm David, by the way," he added by way of introduction as he offered his hand to her.

Samantha smiled, "Of course, you are."

The stranger seemed perplexed. "I can show you my passport if you wish," he joked with her.

"Sorry, no I just mean, of course your name is David."

"Any why, of course?" He felt confused by the conversation.

"It's a long story," was all Samantha shared as she bowed her head in despair.

"Would you like to tell me this long story over a coffee maybe?" he encouraged her.

Samantha looked at the kind stranger and a sense of loneliness washed over her.

"Sure, why not," she eagerly agreed. "Let's go, I know this nice little cafe, just over the next canal bridge."

SEVEN

Piazza San Marco, Venice

Samantha spilled the entire story to her newfound friend. She explained the random meeting in Rome and the knowledge that she somehow knew the handsome tour guide and then the realisation of who he actually was, being the stranger from Hanoi. It was a relief for Samantha to finally share the whole story with someone. She had decided up until now not to tell anyone back home what had been happening. The truth of the situation was that Samantha could hardly believe for herself that she had once again found her David.

"So, what do you think?" she asked her companion. "Do you believe in soulmates?"

He was quick to respond with his own ponderings on the not so random meetings between two strangers.

"Soulmates, as in the person you were always meant to meet?" Samantha clarified.

"Well I like to think of soulmates in a much broader context than that. A soulmate can take many forms. Soulmates can be those friends who you journey through life with. You know, those people that you can't imagine not having in your life. And a soulmate can come in the form of a pet for some. Dogs for example as a perfect example of an animal soulmate and then of course, there is the soulmate that steals our hearts. The person that you meet and you know you need to spend the rest of your life with."

Samantha was listening intently. "That is just beautiful. I love that definition. I don't think I had thought of soulmates in quite that way before." She paused to think further about how this definition fitted for her own situation with her very own David.

"Do you think each person has only one romantic soulmate?" Her interest in the topic was piqued by this new concept of a very old term.

"That my dear… is the billion-dollar question."

Samantha laughed. "I always thought the saying was million-dollar question."

"Inflation," her sensible new friend responded.

Samantha was thoughtful. She thoroughly enjoyed having the conversation with a stranger she stumbled upon in a chance meeting. She could honestly share her thoughts without fear of judgement. In reality, her story about how her and David had come to be a couple was so unbelievable that she had been reluctant to tell anyone about it.

"How did you get so wise?" she asked David number two.

"Not so wise, I don't think. I just have had time to contemplate such things."

Samantha was feeling more and more confident that this handsome tourist had a wealth of information and ideas to share with her. She felt courageous enough to tell him the latest and most concerning development to their relationship. She explained David's sudden departure and how even with several attempts to contact him, she hadn't heard a single word in return.

David number two was hesitant to create any hypothesis around the absence of a reply, especially given that it seemed out of character to her lover's previous behaviour to date. At least, out of character from his behaviour as Samantha had explained it to him. He asked Samantha what she thought it all meant.

"I don't know. I don't want to think it means anything adverse. That would be too much to imagine. But something doesn't feel right about it. I sometimes have a fleeting panicked thought that

David changed his mind about us. I try to push that to the back of my mind because I just don't truly believe that could be the reason."

"So…" David number two encouraged her to continue her thought.

"I have an even greater dread that something has happened to his mother. As in she may not have recovered. It seems to me to be the only logical explanation. It feels absolutely abhorrent to come to that conclusion but it is the only one that makes sense at the moment."

Samantha's phone rung. It was David. She hurried to answer it, breathing heavily into the microphone as the excitement to see his name on the screen took her breath away.

"David?" she answered.

Samantha was overjoyed to hear his voice. She wanted nothing more than to speak to him. David took the time to explain to Samantha what had happened. Everything from the fall his mother took while trying to paint, to the long wait in the hospital for her to open her eyes, to the final heartbreaking decision to turn off the life support to his ailing mother.

Tears fell from Samantha's eyes. She heard every word with the pained expression of a man heartbroken. She tried not to let that familiar feeling of loss well up inside her as hearing the death of a parent triggered for her the painful memory at the loss of her own father. She tried to remain focused on the needs of her lover in that present moment.

"David, I am so, so, sorry for you." Her heart broke for him as she tore the words from her mouth. "What can I do for you? Can I come to you?"

"I am sorry Sam. I just need some time here. Time here with my family to process all of this."

He paused as if not knowing what the time would do for him. Knowing full well it would never bring his mother back. Never again would they be a complete family.

"Sam, do you understand?" he asked her for compassion once more.

"Of course, David." She wanted to hold him. She wanted to be there for him, but she had to respect his wishes. "You just let me know if and when I can be there for you…ok?" She encouraged his agreement to her plea.

"Yes, of course." Samantha could hear he was getting ready to say goodbye.

"David?"

"Yes Sam?"

"I love you!"

"I love you more than you could ever imagine," David replied.

Samantha placed the phone down and let the tears flow. She allowed the stranger, her new friend to warmly embrace her in an attempt to comfort her. David number two felt like a guardian angel sent directly to her to help her through this time of need. The shock at hearing David's softly spoken and heartbreaking words tore at her heart. What a tragedy for him, for the whole family to lose their mother in such a senseless way.

Sam's tears brought back the persistent cough that had continued to plague her. She reached for the last of her wine to soothe the dry, sharp pain each new eruption in her throat caused. Her chest felt heavy. The wine didn't soothe and her throat felt tight and restricted. She couldn't stop coughing and David handed her his glass of wine to finish as well.

"That is a terrible cough you have there. Do you need to see a doctor about it?"

Samantha tried to capture her breath once more as she looked at her companion with displeasure. She hated anytime anyone mentioned a medical visit to her and probably even more so now given David's tragic news.

"No, but thanks for the thought. I might have to head back now," Samantha suggested.

"Can I walk you back to your hotel, just to make sure you are ok?" her new friend asked.

"Thanks," she agreed.

Samantha crawled into bed alone and lonely once again. She wanted nothing more than to have David beside her. She wanted nothing more than to be with him in his time of need. She hated being so far away and felt helpless to do anything to ease his pain. Samantha felt the tears well again and cried into the pillow. The tears flowed fast as she thought about the anguish her lover must be feeling.

* * *

The next morning was an early start to get to the airport in Venice via boat shuttle to catch her plane to Paris. Once again, Samantha wished David was beside her but had always envisaged making this trip on her own. It would be her first time in Paris and she had some reservations about how she might enjoy it.

The boat pulled up with careful precision and the kind captain offered a hand with her luggage up the thin wooden plank. Samantha settled in the front of the boat for the hour-long journey to the airport. She thought again about the conversation with the David number two from the Piazza San Marco and his idea of soulmates. The concepts made perfect sense to Samantha. Long ago her and her twin sister, Sarah had acknowledged their soulmate connection.

Fated since conception to journey their lives together, the sisters had been best friends. How then, Samantha wondered, can a soulmate destined to walk alongside for a lifetime, end up being lost so tragically. Could Sarah have really been Samantha's twin soulmate if she chose to leave her when Samantha needed her the most? The grief at her loss, triggered so much anger inside her that her chest caught in a sharp pain. There were no tears when Samantha thought of her sister's death. Although lost years earlier, her mourning for her sister had still not begun. There was simply no conceivable way to begin to mourn the loss of your twin.

With David never far from her mind, Samantha once more turned her attention to the idea of a romantic soulmate, someone destined to meet, always and forever ordained to be your partner in life. And to anyone that might hear it, hers and David's story as incredible as it was, would seem just that. Soulmates, fated to find one another. She was grateful that she had made the trip to Rome. Thankful for taking the tour and blessed beyond comprehension that she found her David once more.

Every thought of him ripped at her heart. She looked out over the blue waters of Venice and imagined what he might be doing.

* * *

Back home in Los Angeles, David tied his tie and glanced into the mirror briefly to ensure it was straight. He was simply going through the motions of getting dressed. Not thinking about what was to come but simply performing the necessary robotic motions of putting one shoe on after the other. His father had struggled to wake and David had found himself on the edge of his father's bed holding his sobbing parent. Caleb was taking care of the practical arrangements of ensuring the appropriate people had confirmed their understanding of their assigned roles for the day.

The day that would change their lives forever. Not having had the time to come to grips with the loss of a much-loved woman, today was their chance to say their final farewells. The fact that his mother never gained consciousness meant that thankfully she did not suffer in pain, but it also meant that not only David, but his father and brother never got the chance to tell her one more time, how much they loved her.

Today he would say those words and hope that wherever she was, she would hear him.

The service was a small one at his father's request. Only a handful of close family and friends were invited to join the men in their sad farewell. Flowers adorned the casket, as did photos from loved ones who wanted to share a small token of a lifetime of wonderful memories.

Caleb took to the front of the room to speak. He had prepared a selection of photos and videos to share as a celebration of his mother's life. The crowd were in tears as they viewed the moments shared together. Finally, it was time for David to take his place before the gathering of friends to speak.

"I want to say something that feels truly significant for me on this day." He paused. These were the most difficult words he had been forced to speak in his life to date.

"The love of a mother is truly unlike anything else. She is the one person who knows the privilege of carrying her children through pregnancy. Destined to grow within her womb, her children are afforded their own privilege of hearing their mother's heartbeat from inside her body. This bond doesn't wither with time nor age. Instead growing stronger with every year. I couldn't have asked for a more caring mother. I will miss her every day. Please take your loved ones in your arms today and tell them one more time, no, tell them endless times how much you love them. Never stop telling them. For one day it will be the last time they will hear those words. One day, and for my family today is that day, there are no words left to be said except, I love you Mum."

Tears fell freely in the small room. David turned to see his father huddled in his brother's arms. The word that kept coming into his mind was time. The only thought was of the importance of time and of not wasting it. Not wasting a second of his life again. Not for a moment forgetting the gift of a lifetime, often so much shorter than we would have hoped for. Death was once more the great leveller - nothing and no one could avoid it. At the end of life, we have left just two special gifts, our memories and our loved ones, and David was determined to cherish them both.

He knew what he needed to do. He needed to get back to his Samantha. He wanted to hold her in his arms and tell her how much he loved her and how he never wanted to be apart from her again.

Eight

Paris, France

Paris greeted Samantha with a cold and rainy welcome. She was surprised at the ease of finding a cab and passing on directions to the top floor apartment she had rented for two weeks. She grinned at the memory of her discussion with her landlord, Kay, an Australian woman, Sydney based. A talented and creative spirit, a theatre actor. Samantha had shared her desire to rent the tiny one-bedroom apartment on Rue de Clery in the second arrondissement of the world-famous city of love.

Kay had quizzed Samantha and was curious about the Australian blogger travelling solo through Europe. When Samantha said she wanted to write her blogs on the balcony of the delightful apartment, Kay jumped at the chance and booked her the space. Her landlord was particular about who she rented her quiet, little Parisian home to when she wasn't there. The women shared stories and connected through their love of the arts. Kay was so taken by the passion of Samantha's creative inspiration she made her a solemn promise.

Working tirelessly on the upcoming stage production of Zanadu had inspired Kay's creative powers. She made the promise to send Samantha a muse. A magical muse who would inspire and stir the creative fervour within. A muse to ignite creativity, stir the senses and entice wonderful mystical words to appear on the page. Samantha was excited at the prospect and wondered what form the muse would take.

He didn't take long to appear. He appeared in the form of an Irish photographer, a friend of Kays who had the inevitable task of carrying Samantha's heavy bag the five flights of stairs to the tiny apartment. Once there he was to provide a tour including how to work the heater, an essential in Paris in the middle of winter, and hand over the key. An hour later of getting to know each other and Samantha was none the wiser on the heating, nor the household rules.

The two stood, Seamus with his back against the kitchen bench, a wide grin as he asked Samantha one question after another about her travels. Samantha stood directly across, leaning against the kitchen bench curious about her muse; his art, his travel and why he had chosen to call Paris home.

The connection and the comfort were instant. The curiosity about the other was real and the two immediately identified key interests and commonalities.

"Well, I better show you around then," Seamus suggested, possibly suddenly remembering the important tasks at hand. Samantha fell in love with the space, every inch of it, homely and welcoming. It was the perfect choice for her short stay in Paris.

"Hey, do you know anyone in Paris?" Seamus asked after the tour.

"Not a soul," Samantha admitted.

"Want to come out for a drink tonight? I have a photo shoot until about eleven but we can meet after that if you like." Samantha jumped at the chance to spend some more time with her muse.

"Sure, I would love to. Meet you there."

Only a couple of hours in Paris and Samantha already had plans to meet some locals, with the prospect of exciting new adventures with her muse. And the night did not fail to please. Seamus met Samantha at the bar as promised and immediately introduced her to his two good friends, colleagues from his recent stint as a bar attendant at the very place. A quaint local little bar, dark and full of character, strong wooden tables and numerous chairs crowded the small dimly lit space. Seamus and Samantha took pride of place at the bar, laughing with DJ, the six-foot-four giant of a man from Israel, and Mel, the bubbly blonde kiwi chick with a million stories to share.

Samantha's previous sullen mood was transformed by the place and the company. The foursome laughed and shared shots as the bar clientele one by one made their way home for the night. Only a few stragglers were left when DJ called last drinks. The locals knew the procedure well with Paris city licensing only allowing bars to stay open until two a.m. Samantha imagined she would need to make a move as well when Mel assured her that friends were allowed to stay long after the bar closed.

And true to her word, DJ, Mel, Seamus, Samantha and two other regulars were permitted to stay as the last curtain was drawn and the lights were dimmed. A tourist from the Czech Republic was rushed along to finish his drink. He had been taken by Mel and was reluctant to leave, wanting instead as he stated in slurred heavily accented words, "To stay and get to know the beautiful and confident Kiwi girl called Mel."

Samantha laughed at the cheesiness of his drunken pick up line. He was obsessed and Samantha did her best to distract Mel and save her from the obvious unwanted attention of the tourist.

"Come on, drink up now," Mel encouraged the tourist.

He looked around to see that others weren't being hurried along in the same way.

"But they stay?" he asked in his best English.

Mel sighed, feeling tired and now slightly irritable at this insistence on delaying his departure. "Yes, they can stay because they are friends, friends can stay but the bar has to close. It's the law."

He looked displeased but with a sense of hope in his eyes. "But, I a friend to Mel," he insisted.

The few remaining regulars at the bar erupted in laughter. DJ sensed it was his time to intervene and with a friendly hand on the man's back he ushered him to the door, removing his glass from his hand as he did.

"Come on mate," DJ encouraged him. "Time to go. It's the law. The bar has to close."

"But I friend of Mel," the tourist repeated, determined in his mission to stay close by and try to spend just a few more minutes around the friendly blonde bar attendant.

DJ persisted in his removal and closed the door behind the tourist.

The bar calmed once more and the final curtains closed for the friends to share a shot of their latest concoction in peace. Just as the shots were poured, the door swung open and the luckless tourist again began pleading his case to stay. DJ was quick this time to respond and on reaching the man, again stated that friends only can drink after the two a.m. deadline.

The tourist looked hurt, his eyes fell, his loneliness obvious. DJ stood his hand on his shoulder ready to guide him gently to the door. Taking pity on the solo traveller, DJ offered another form of reasoning.

"Look mate, this is a gang bang. We are gang bangers so you can't stay."

The tourist through his drunken stupor saw a ray of light and immediately began removing his jacket that had been placed on just moments earlier to depart into the cold winter night.

"I do gang bang!" he proudly announced to the bar as he removed the final sleeve of his dark, woolen jacket. "I gang banger," he added as the bar lost any resemblance of composure and erupted into even louder fits of laughter.

DJ took a step back as he himself found it impossible not to laugh. The tourist, encouraged that he was now allowed entry, found the buttons on his shirt, trying but fumbling to remove the clothing from his body. His eyes worked the room, obviously calculating the numbers in the bar; two lone local men at the end of the bar, DJ the gentle giant and Seamus the stocky Irishman. He turned his eyes to the two girls, the blonde Aussie, Samantha and the woman of his desires, the outrageously spoken, gorgeous Mel. He liked his odds. He was going to make this work one way or another.

Seamus placed his palm on the small of Samantha's back, letting her know she was in no danger and he was there to protect her. Mel, standing inside the bar, the palm of both hands leaning down in tired desperation spoke up.

"Enough already," she demanded.

DJ composed himself as the man began work on his second button.

"Come on mate, you can't gang bang here. This is a friends' only gang bang," he joked with him once more."

"I gang bang friend of Mel," the star-struck tourist pleaded his case once more.

The bar couldn't help but laugh. Mel tried hard to hide her embarrassment at the unwanted attention and decided to put an end to the humorous prank.

"That's enough, put him out already," she instructed DJ who silently picked up the tourist's jacket and assisted him to the door once more. Closing it behind them, the friends fell into fits of laughter at the persistence of the tourist.

The shots were finally offered and the four friends poured the warm, delicious liquid down their throats as the two local men finished their beers, said their goodbyes and made for the door.

Just then, the heavy wooden door opened again. This time the tourist appeared phone in hand, searching, scrolling for some vital piece of information. He opened his mouth to speak, the foursome attentive to the obviously important question the tourist had to ask.

"This gang bang…" he began, "is it live streamed?"

Barely able to hold back the laughter, DJ took his place beside the tourist once more and walked him directly to the door.

"No," he answered him. "No live streaming." The door closed one final time as Mel loudly instructed,

"And would someone lock that fucking door already!"

The night continued for another three hours as the four new friends shared laughter and shots. They told stories of their homelands and shared a humorous video of the Aussie hero who busted his plugger while chasing an armed robber. As five a.m. rolled around the friends quietly closed the bar and made their way to the back entrance, locking it carefully as they left before hugging each other goodbye. Seamus ensured Samantha was safely in her Uber before he made his way by bike to his one-bedroom unit for some much-deserved rest.

Samantha made it home and miraculously up the five-steep flight of stairs before climbing into her new bed for the night. She was thankful that she followed the heating instructions as offered to her and the apartment was a perfect toasty temperature for a long and restful sleep. Her final thoughts were of her soulmate as she wondered how he was and when she would see him again. She fell asleep imagining his warm body next to her.

The next morning, her first stop was the required visit to the city's most famous landmark, the Eiffel Tower. She managed to capture some interesting photos and was happy to be back in her room later that night to download the images to her laptop.

She watched the images upload and flash quickly before her eyes, one at a time. She took a good look at each one to see if there was anything of value in the batch. Finding a few choice shots, she was happy with the day's work and decided she would reward herself with some non-essential social media updates. The blogger's most dreaded distraction was the numerous and active social media outlets, each one capable of wasting hours of a busy day.

She took a quick look at David's socials pages to see if by chance he had updated the world as to his loss. As expected not a word, the page hadn't been touched for weeks. Not added to since before meeting Samantha, strangely enough. Or not so strange given that they had barely a moment apart since they met and before David was urgently rushed away.

Desperate for a reminder of the beautiful man she loved, Samantha went once more to the collection of albums on her laptop. She slowly and methodically indulged her desire with images of her gorgeous David. She missed him so much she felt a pain in her chest at his absence. She touched her finger to the screen and pressed it lightly to the lips that she craved. She wondered when she would feel his lips on hers once more.

A tone alerted her to a message on her phone. She smiled as she recognised the name. It was from her soulmate.

I am missing you. Where in the world can I find you? Love David

Samantha was quick to respond.

I miss you and can't wait to see you again. I am in Paris. Love you more!

The next message was instant.

I will join you in a couple of days and not possible! I love you more than you could ever imagine.

Samantha leapt from the large bed and danced and cheered into the silence of the lonely room. She was overjoyed to be seeing him again. She could hardly wait the hours to hold him once more.

* * *

Waking early the next morning, barely able to sleep at the thought of her beautiful David joining her in the City of Love, Samantha quickly headed out to explore more of the passionate city that was Paris.

Taking in the sights and the sounds of the Champs de Elysees, Samantha paused for a moment as she approached the Arch De Triomph. She had seen its impressive image hundreds of times before but nothing could prepare her for the feelings that it evoked standing in its magnificence. The final resting place of the unknown soldier; a burial site acknowledged and respected by opposing troops, enemies and friends alike. This was the grave of the soldier said to represent all those who came before him and all of those who should follow.

Samantha raised her camera to the sun and attempted to capture the imposing structure in the frame. Her passion for photography far outweighed her talent for it and she lowered the screen to assess the worthiness of the image. She sighed with defeat at the enormity of the task. Evoking an emotion from an image that she could see but failed to capture.

She noticed a fellow photographer on the corner of the path. His camera raised to the structure. His pose steady and sure, she watched as he too lowered his screen to view his creation. Samantha couldn't help but be curious as to his findings. She walked toward him, tapped him on the shoulder and courageously introduced herself.

"Hi, I'm Samantha." She offered her hand in greeting.

He was taken aback and took a few moments to assess this unusually friendly individual before him.

"Hello, I'm Seamus," he replied in his thick Irish accent.

Samantha blushed, slightly embarrassed. "Sorry, I didn't recognise you under all those clothes."

Seamus couldn't help but laugh, "There's an invite if I have ever heard one."

Samantha giggled at the awkwardness of the situation. "I meant the beanie and scarf and jacket. I only saw you from behind." She hoped her explanation would suffice. "I just noticed you taking a photo of the Arch and wondered if I could see what it looked like."

Seamus stood staring at her, wondering what her strange request was about.

"Really?"

Samantha continued addressing his hesitation. "My photos are pathetic and I wanted to see what a professional photographer's photos look like of the same image."

Seamus was still hesitant to share with his friend, his latest artistic offerings.

"Samantha?" he responded, "I'm sure my photos are no better than yours." He appeared shy to share his work.

Samantha was despondent. She had hoped to find inspiration from her muse and wanted to see his images as he took them, but as an artist she had to appreciate the process and respect his wishes.

"Would you like to have a drink and share images? I'll show you mine, if you show me yours?" He teased her a little, a giant grin forming on his attractive face.

"Um, I'm not sure…" Her voice trailed off.

He felt bad for making a joke at her expense. "Stop, Samantha. I am sorry. That wasn't polite of me. Of course, I will show you. But I wasn't kidding. I would be interested in seeing what you captured too."

Samantha smiled as the relief washed over her. "Ok, let's get a drink and share then."

As they settled in the small café, Samantha was awe struck at the beauty of the images before her. It was nearly impossible to believe that two cameras at the same place could take such very different photos. She stared more closely at the small screen of the camera. The sky a perfect shade of blue, the Arch defined by its solid stone structure imposing a defining line in the clouds behind it. She could only dream of creating an image so spectacular.

"How do you do it?" She was curious to improve, to learn from this master of visual delight.

"It is all about the lighting," he assured her. "You have to consider the lighting you are working with and adjust accordingly. If you have a bright cloudless sky you have something different to work with than if you have a cloudy grey sky." Samantha listened intently to his words of wisdom. "And if you want to evoke an emotion, you can use the surrounds to capture that without the use of too much enhancing."

Viewing the image once more, the white clouds on the bright blue backdrop demanded as much of one's focus as the Arch itself. It was as if the Arch, the man-made construct was forced to take a back stage to the magnificence of nature's formation of majestic clouds across the skyline.

Samantha could understand and comprehend his words but the ability to capture such inspiration still evaded her.

"I try, but it doesn't appear on the image the same as I see with my eyes or imagine it could look."

Seamus smiled a knowing smile at her, a smile that saw through her and created a comfort between them. "You just have to trust yourself. It will come," he insisted.

The two creative souls joined for drinks, laughter and conversation long into the night. They had covered religion, philosophy, psychology, quantum psychics and family before they finally turned to the subject of soulmates, a subject close to Samantha's heart. She was curious to find out what this creative spirit felt about the concept of soulmates.

He looked surprised at the question as if never considering it before. Samantha was silent. She didn't want to prompt a response, instead content to wait for this brilliant mind before her to formulate a representation of a soulmate from his own belief system.

Samantha waited patiently. She had been taking in every piece of advice and wisdom she could conjure to try to help her make sense of this somewhat spiritual connection with David.

Finally, Seamus began to speak. "I don't know what to say about soulmates. I don't think I know. I am not sure I would know if I met mine. I guess I don't really believe that you have only one person that is your soulmate. I think you can love many people in one lifetime."

Samantha felt sad for him. This creative genius who lived so passionately through his work yet hadn't experienced the great passion and pain that comes from connection with your romantic soulmate. The lack of affirmation confirmed for Samantha what she already knew. She knew that a person who had met their soulmate could never doubt it. They could never be unsure as to what it meant or how to recognise it. For Samantha, meeting David and realising instantly that she knew his eyes, knew his soul was confirmation enough for her. She suddenly had the most urgent desire to see her soulmate again.

Seamus spoke again, having considered the concept a little further he had more to add. "I think I believe in soulmates that appear as friends and family. I guess that's what I mean when I say that you can love more than one person in a lifetime. There are just too many possibilities and different types of relationships for any one person to be the destined one and only one for another."

He looked to Samantha, who appeared to be emotional at hearing the declaration.

"Did I say something wrong?" he coerced her.

She was hesitant to disagree with his logic, "No, not at all. It's just that I feel so lost at the moment, but not in a good way. When you travel and know that around each corner is a new experience, well I love that kind of lost anticipation. But at the moment I just feel so unsure of everything. I don't enjoy the feeling at all."

Seamus nodded, he knew the feeling well. Having been born in Ireland and grown up surrounded by a close family before deciding to venture out and travel the world, finally calling Paris home for the last decade. He too, a free spirit destined to continue to travel, meeting new people and exploring new places all the time. He understood completely that addictive feeling of venturing into the unknown. He nodded as he allowed Samantha to continue with her thoughts.

"I just feel without direction right now, I'm not sure why I keep questioning myself. I thought I had found my home. I thought I had found my soulmate but things haven't been as easy as I had hoped."

Seamus threw his head back in a knowing laughter, not to belittle Samantha's words of concern, but in a joining of understanding at the words he heard.

"Samantha, can I share with you one of the greatest lessons I have learnt?" He paused waiting for confirmation that she actually wanted to hear more from him.

"Of course, Seamus. I am soaking up every ounce of your wisdom." She was keen to expand her own concepts and test her existing beliefs and this confident and generous soul was eager to assist her.

He smiled at the compliment. He felt protective of this vulnerable, sensitive creature who appeared out of nowhere to challenge his world for a short time. He looked at his watch and realised they had been talking constantly for several hours. It had felt like minutes. This, he thought to himself is a sign of meeting a soulmate, when you are in their company and time flies. You lose yourself so much in the other person that time no longer seems to exist.

Seamus dared not share this thought with his new friend. She appeared to be struggling enough already with her fledgling new romance to want to hear the possibility of another soulmate connection. He returned to his original thought and shared with Samantha one of his life's most important lessons.

"I learnt a while ago, that life wasn't meant to be easy and the worst thing someone like you or me can do is to expect easy. Think about it, Samantha..." he continued. "How did we ever acquire the ideal that life was meant to be easy and hurdles are a negative byproduct of some tragedy in an otherwise perfect world?"

Samantha listened intently at this new concept to challenge her belief system.

Seamus took this as a sign to continue. "Answer me this Samantha… did anyone ever promise you that life was going to be easy? Trouble free?" He waited for a response. "When you were young, did your parents ever say, this is life, it is going to be perfect and brilliant and you will love every minute of it. It is not possible is it. For without the lows how do you feel the highs, without the unbridled sadness how do you know what unimaginable happiness feels like. It is the balance of life that allows us to feel each minute of it exactly as we are meant to."

Samantha's eyes shot skyward as her mind searched her memory for the correct answer. She was the first to acknowledge what an amazing childhood she had and knew that she was privileged to be born into the family she was. She hadn't really experienced any real hardship in life. Her first real hurdle was the death of her beloved father and even that was something that her father ensured was as painless as possible for her with his words of comfort and strength to her.

The memory of her beloved twin, a loss following the death of their father, began to find its way to her conscious brain and she violently pushed the thought back down. It wasn't time to think of Sarah yet. She still wasn't ready. The emotion was still too raw.

Samantha searched her mind further and questioned why it was that hurdles and difficulties were seen as unexpected complications instead of part and parcel of life. Seamus was right, no one had ever promised an easy life, so why was it that so many people had come to think of hardship in this way.

Finally, she looked toward her new friend with her answer. She searched his face for clues as to the origin of this brilliant mind. She wondered again how he was so wise. She imagined a life well lived. An individual didn't acquire this level of insight and compassion unless they too have lived through tragedy and despair. She wondered if this was part of the reason Seamus had chosen to leave his family behind at such a young age to travel the world alone for the rest of his life.

Seamus was silent as he waited patiently for Samantha's response.

"No," Samantha finally agreed. "No one every promised an easy life. I don't know why I felt that was what was owed to me. Actually, I feel kind of ashamed for thinking that the whole time." She let the new thought sink in further. She felt guilty at how good her life had been and how much she had let such small things become big issues. Her thoughts turned to the plight of refugees, to the homeless, to those who suffered great hardships and lived through it.

This was the great fortune that came to those who travel. It was the chance meeting in a foreign country with a stranger that changed your belief system. The interactions that you could never have envisaged that become part of the fabric of the ever-growing person that the traveller becomes. You wake in the morning, strap a camera around your neck searching for inspiration for writing and suddenly a new possibility appears and life is never the same.

Samantha remembered back to her life-changing reunion with David. There was no way either one of them could have known what the night would bring as they drank their morning coffee. Great possibility came from the openness to explore worlds unknown.

The soulmate journey, Samantha giggled as she conjured up a new name for her current collection of blogs. Soulmates… she thought again and glanced once more to the attractive and philosophical Irishman in front of her. How easily she could have imagined Seamus to be her soulmate. How true were his words to her that a person has more than one soulmate? If Samantha hadn't met David again just a couple of weeks earlier, she would definitely have wanted to spend more time with this attractive creative.

Seamus smiled at her as if reading her mind. He laughed a little.

"What is behind that smile?" she insisted, somewhat embarrassed at her own thoughts.

"I think I know what you are thinking."

"God, I hope not!" was Samantha's firm response.

"Haha," he laughed a knowing laugh. "Yeah I felt it too." He paused for reassurance that she wasn't going to take his next words wrongly. "I think a few days ago, I met one of my soulmates too." He smiled a knowing smile and leaned toward her to kiss her lightly on the left cheek.

"Seamus… I…" she stammered.

"Don't worry. I understand," he assured her quickly. "I know you have met your 'one'. I just wanted you to know that I feel something here too." He paused once more and wanted to confirm her understanding of his intent, "Friends?"

This time he held out his palm for a handshake. Samantha smiled with relief and took his hand.

"Friends," she agreed.

Samantha kissed Seamus goodnight as the two made the promise to keep in contact. She had enjoyed the effortless company of this creative spirit and had hoped they might meet again in the not too distant future.

As Samantha made her way back to her little Parisian apartment she walked the cobblestone streets as if for the first time she knew who she was in the world. This paradise of creative contentment made her feel at home. The narrow pathways, the uneven surfaces, each of them feeling just as they should. Samantha felt a sense of certainty about what she wanted and sense of confidence that her wildest dreams were within her grasp.

She skipped over the puddle that beckoned her demise. She laughed as the rain startled to drizzle on her sunny disposition. Nothing was going to make her feel anything other than absolute joy.

She had found him. She had found her soulmate and she was determined now that she was never going to let him get away again.

* * *

Caleb begged his brother once more to stay. "David, you can't leave him now. He needs us."

"You don't understand. I can't stand to be without her one more second. This just proves that we don't have time to waste. Doesn't our mother's death mean anything to you?"

"Mean to me? How do you have the audacity to say that to me? I have been here with Dad from the minute this happened. I have been the son who tried to stay close to be there, when they needed me. I haven't been perfect but I have been a hundred times better than you," Caleb spat back at his brother.

"Don't you give me your guilt trip." David sized up his brother. He wasn't able to hear reason. He just needed to get back to his Samantha.

Caleb stood down. He lowered his head and sighed. "Do what you have to do," he tried to reassure his brother.

David saw the anguish in Caleb's face. Instantly he recognised the raw emotion that had been fuelling his little brother's passionate plea.

"I am sorry Caleb, you are right. You have been the responsible one."

Caleb looked hopefully into David's eyes. "Dad needs us now. We need to be here."

David nodded in agreement as Caleb continued.

"If she is the one, she will still be there. She will understand."

David's chest heaved as his heart wept for his love. He wanted to hold her close. To never let her go. He wanted to make sure she was safe. He couldn't lose her too. Not now. Not ever.

"I will stay," David reassured his brother. "Our father needs us both now. And we need each other." The brothers shared a familiar embrace and a promise to care for the little family they had left.

The boys' father entered the room just as they released each other from their sacred promise. He wept as he watched them.

"You boys miss her too?" He looked to their faces for comfort.

The brothers walked slowly the few short steps to their fragile parent. Caleb was first to speak, "We will miss her with all of our hearts Dad."
Once more their father fell into their arms. His grief taking its toll on his exhausted spirit. The brothers helped their father to a chair and sat with him while he gathered his thoughts. He needed to talk. He needed to tell his sons how much he missed their mother.

He smiled at the renewed love for his wife. "Have I ever told you about the first time I knew I loved your mother?" He smiled longingly into the faces of his two children.

David smiled back, knowing the story word for word. He could not deny his father this magical trip down memory lane. "Tell us again Dad…how did you know mum was the one?"

The three men sat as tears formed in their already reddened eyes. Their father spoke of a love that was certain; a love that never faltered, a love that the two younger men had only ever imagined possible in another's lifetime.

"And do you know what?" their father asked of them. Not waiting for permission to continue, he added, "Once I knew she was the one, I never wanted to let her out of my sight." Their father dropped his head, his hands rose to his eyes and covered his tears as they fell abundantly. "I should never have left her alone that day!"

Caleb was the first to comfort his father, cradling him in his arms as the older man wept without pride or discomfort. Caleb held his father tightly and rocked him as he sobbed uncontrollably. He looked to David, mesmerised by his father's words and uttered to him.

"You should go to her. Don't let her out of your sight."

These were the words David longed to hear. He needed his brother's permission to be released from his responsibilities to find once more the woman he loved. He paused his enthusiasm to look toward his family, now a quarter of the size smaller than just a few weeks earlier. The sudden departure of just one human being made the most devastating impact on this tiny family unit.

Caleb looked once more to his brother. "I am sure Dad will understand," he whispered quietly. He longed for his brother to share the love that his father had just lost. He wanted nothing more than for some happiness and joy, some meaning to come from this senseless loss.

David felt the heaviness in his chest as he allowed the words to escape his lips. "No… my place is here for now."

Caleb nodded. He knew his brother would stay with them and he believed that his lover would wait until one day soon when the grief of their loss had plunged into the darkest recesses of their souls. The boys couldn't leave until their father's grief found its way to the shallow waters of acceptance. Only then would the brothers part and allow their father time to grieve on his own.

Morning came around once more and as David had prepared for his departure, he now had to prepare for the devastating realisation that he wouldn't see Samantha again soon. He only hoped that she understood the position he was in. He felt sure that she would, given the loss of her own father just a few years before.

He prepared to phone, not quite sure what to say. Not wanting to say anything to the woman he loved but that he would be with her soon, but that would be a lie.

* * *

Samantha had been counting the hours until she held her David in her arms once more. Her phone rang and she was excited to speak to him to hear how much longer she needed to wait. His tone was pensive.

"Sam…" he paused.

"Yes?" She sensed something was wrong with her lover.

"I am so sorry but I can't join you this week. My Dad…" David couldn't continue for as much as he needed to be there for his father, he also needed for himself to be close to Samantha.
Samantha didn't let him say another word.

"I understand. You don't need to explain to me. Please." Her heart broke as she acknowledged the pain her lover was in. "Can I come to you? I want to be there for you."

David contemplated for a moment what it would mean to have Samantha close to him, to his family. To be there with them as they worked their way through the minefield that was their sudden loss of their mother and wife.

"I would love nothing more, but…" he didn't want to discourage Samantha's enthusiasm or sense of belonging in his family, but he knew now wasn't the time for her to be with them.

"Sam…" He paused again, not quite sure how to let her know.

"David… I understand." She didn't want him to struggle with the words to explain his predicament. "I will be here for you, whenever you need me. Just know that." She paused before adding, "I love you David."

"I love you more than you could ever imagine!" David replied.

Samantha smiled a huge smile. She had never heard a declaration of love so certain, so promising, so infinite.

"David, just promise me, whenever you need me, wherever you need me, just call and I will be there."

"I know!" David had to tear himself from her. "I have to go now. Love you," he added one final time before ending the call.

Samantha held the phone to her ear just a second more, longing to hear his voice one final time. Her heart and her head were at battle. She just wanted to jump on the next plane and be with her David. She wanted to kiss him better and heal his wounds. She wanted to be with his family. But she stayed in place on the chair she was in and just held the phone to her ear. In that moment, she feared she may never hold her David again.

Nine

Paris, France

Samantha received an unexpected call from her publishing house in London. They wanted to talk to her about her progress in converting her blogs into a travel book. In David's absence she agreed to make the short trip to talk to them about her latest creative offerings. As always, she had left arrangements to the last minute and as she stood outside in the drizzling rain, she glanced at her watch once more.

The taxi was uncharacteristically late. She looked at the time on her phone and with some quick calculations realised that if the taxi didn't arrive within the next ten minutes, she would surely miss her train.

Samantha waited and hoped for a miracle. And he came, his name was Walter and as he arrived he jumped out of the car and apologised to Samantha for his lateness.

"Have you been waiting long?" he asked. "Forty minutes maybe?" He had hoped this wasn't the case.

Samantha was attempting to remain calm even though she was increasingly panicked at missing her train and her best opportunity yet at getting her blogs published. "It's ok, just that I need to get to the train station in the next thirty minutes."

"What time is your boarding?" he asked her as a matter of course.

"Ten o'clock," she let him know.

He finally took her bag and placed it into the boot of the taxi for her. He started the car, indicated and slowly made his careful pull away from the curb. Samantha felt her heart sink in her chest as she realised that her casual response to the meeting had caused her to potentially miss it altogether. She cursed herself for her disorganisation.

The driver was smiling without a care in the world and Samantha became curious as to what was behind the smile.

"Have you always lived here, in Paris?" she asked him after detecting a different accent in his voice, German perhaps, slightly diluted by living in various places maybe.

He seemed pleased to be asked. "For the last five years, yes, before that I lived in Munich. Except for the year I spent in Central America."

Samantha felt a story coming, "What were you doing in Central America, if you don't mind me asking?"

The taxi driver seemed happy to continue. "I had a personal crisis. I had a calling to go to Central America to travel and meditate," he added. He spoke slowly and purposefully as if every word was intentional and necessary for the telling of the narrative. "My life is now pre and post. It has been broken up by my year in Central America and what I learnt there."

Samantha was fascinated. Human behaviour had always intrigued her and that morning with the asking of one simple question, this stranger's story of his journey began to unfold. She listened as he told her about the day he was robbed by a stranger with a machete. He spoke calmly; no malice for the perpetrator, no sense of fear for his own safety or re-triggering from the event that would leave a lesser man potentially scarred for life.

He spoke of the man who robbed him of all his possessions. As Walter walked down an unknown street in a small village in Central America, he was confronted by the stranger wielding a full-sized machete and yelling directions in the few English words he appeared to know. Instinctually knowing it safest to obey, Walter placed everything he owned on the ground beneath him before taking a few steps backward. The stranger not losing Walter from his line of sight bent down to gather everything before him.

Watching on with relief as the armed stranger began to walk away, Walter could do nothing but stand and stare. He was simply bewildered as to what had just happened and what his next step should be to try to find his way to safety. The armed stranger walked just a few metres away to examine the contents of the bag and wallet he had just demanded for his own. The man then whistled to draw Walter's attention. Once receiving it, he held up his hand to display to Walter the contents of his clenched fist, being a couple of now crumpled notes of local currency. Walter watched on as the man placed the notes carefully on the ground before him, picked up a rock and placed it on the notes to hold them securely in place. Walter paused in his storytelling at this point to take a breath. The memory of this one moment was quite obviously life changing in nature.

The stranger, machete still in hand was leaving Walter money to catch a bus back to the nearest town. He nodded toward Walter to check his understanding of his visual direction and then turned and walked away, not looking back again. Walter of course grabbed the money as quickly as he could reach it and made his way back to the nearest transport.

"Can you imagine how desperately that man must have needed the cash?" Walter suggested. "To have to resort to robbing me but at odds with his own value for human kindness. It was a defining moment for me."

The two sat in silence for a moment before Samantha asked, "You had no anger toward him? No fear that he would hurt you?"

"There was no time for fear and once I witnessed his gesture of kindness how could I feel anger? This man needed the money more than I did. I will never know what for. Maybe for family? Maybe for medicine, for children who sat days with empty stomachs. He didn't have to leave me anything. He could have left me stranded on the side of the road, but he didn't. He surely could have killed me, but chose not to."

The passenger and the driver continued to share travel stories, speaking of the people they had met and the beauty they had found in the world. They spoke of meditation, veganism, human behaviour, religion and finding yourself.

"You are in a crisis now?" Walter gently suggested to Samantha.

She paused, stunned at the openness of the driver but at the same time thankful that someone had the courage to ask her the all-important question.

"Not a crisis as such," Samantha had to admit. "I just don't know where I belong in the world at the moment nor what my future holds. I wish I knew."

"Is this why you travel now?" he asked her.

"Yes." She paused as she reflected on the enormity of his words. "I am looking for answers, I guess." The emotion in her reply gave way to the persistent irritation in her throat once more and once again the dry, repetitive cough made its way from her throat. The driver's hand left the wheel of the vehicle to offer her a remedy in the form of a Halls, the same lozenge David gave her on their first meeting. She smiled at the coincidence and thanked the stranger for his thoughtfulness.

Samantha looked at the time again. The driver so slow and deliberate in his movements had cars passing him. He spoke with Samantha turning his head often to look at her, not caring so much for the road or the sense of urgency that Samantha had tried to instill in him at the beginning of the trip. But it didn't matter anymore. Samantha felt as if she could speak with this thoughtful and caring older man for hours. She resigned herself to the fact that she was going to miss her train and started to prepare an alternative plan in her head. She checked her phone for any possible flights still available.

The car pulled over. "Here we are," the driver proudly announced. "And with five minutes to spare."

He had done it. He had delivered her directly to the necessary terminal and the exact one with the train she needed to board in clear sight. She had no idea how he even knew to do that.

She hurriedly paid him but stopped herself again from rushing. For this was the lesson for her in the random meeting of like minds.

"Thank you," she said. "I have enjoyed talking with you and I could talk with you for hours more if we had the chance."

"And me with you," Walter added graciously. He stepped out of the car and unloaded Samantha's luggage from the boot for her. As he handed it to her with a smile he stopped to deliver one final important piece of advice.

"Your answers will come." He took her two hands in his. "You just have to stop and breathe."

Samantha smiled. "Thank you!" she replied with genuine gratitude for meeting this inspirational soul. She boarded the train, took her seat and smiled at the great fortune that had been bestowed upon her once again. She felt guilty that the trip was so rushed she didn't even get to ask his last name. Without it, she would have no way to ever repay this thoughtful stranger named Walter for the kind words of inspiration he shared.

The short journey to London was a fortunate one as the publishers encouraged her writing by providing her with another small but promising retainer, enough to keep her travelling for a while longer at least. They had planned to turn Samantha's blog posts into a travel memoir of sorts. Samantha wasn't too sure of the idea of writing entirely from her own experiences and preferred herself to turn it into a work of fiction. A story of lessons learnt, of some greater meaning to life. They agreed to continue the negotiation and come to terms and conditions in a couple of weeks.

Until then Samantha was free to continue blogging and enjoying new experiences in exciting new places.

Arriving back to her small rented apartment in Paris, Samantha wanted nothing more than to share her good news with David, but didn't want to distract him from his own focus right now.

She made the decision to send a text:

Hi David, I hope you are ok. Sending my love to you and your family.

She received a reply only a moment later:

Hi Sam, I love you and wish I could be there. I don't know when I can join you. I love you more than you could ever imagine.

On reading the message the tears flowed freely. Samantha hadn't allowed herself to admit how much she was missing her David and how desperately she needed to see him again. She put her head in her hands and sobbed wildly. After a long while, she fell asleep. She slept alone once more.

Waking to the noise of a celebration outside, Samantha grabbed the blanket from the bed and ventured to the small balcony to open the twin glass doors to step onto the cold concrete outside. She looked down to see a group of four friends joined in obvious celebration, laughing as they walked down the narrow cobbled street beneath her. She remembered back to her night of laughter at the bar with Seamus and his friends.

She stepped back inside to look at the time and although it was already nine in the evening, she assumed that her friend would still be awake. She texted him. Not wanting to be alone again, she craved the company of her muse.

She texted:

Hey Seamus, what are you up to? Want to catch up for a drink? I'm needing a friend to talk to.

Seamus replied:

Would love for you to join us. I am with friends just around the corner from Rue De Clery. We are catching up for some drinks. Come over!

If Samantha had taken a moment to consider it, she would have said no, but instead she jumped at the chance to take her mind off David and meet some new people in this beautiful city she was quickly falling in love with.

Finding the building easily enough, Samantha entered the pin code to allow the huge wooden doors to open onto a perfectly paved and landscaped square courtyard entrance. It was glamorously alight with tiny white fairy lights placed with care to ensure nothing ostentatious, as is the French way to do things, simply and understated.

She made her way to the glass doors leading to the spiral staircase; this seemed to be the architectural favourite of the city, spiral staircases of varying steepness and width. The smaller apartments, the ones Samantha could afford allowed enough space in some places for just one person to ascend the cramped staircase, but this apartment, you could drive a car up the stairs, so wide were they.

Samantha arrived at the door just in time for Seamus to open it with a wide grin, a welcome kiss on the cheek and a glass of bubbly in his hand at the ready for the new guest's arrival. Rather than being the quiet catch up Samantha had anticipated, this gathering marked the homecoming of a joint friend of the combined electric group, the owner of the impressive up-scale Parisian apartment and good friend of Seamus, Tobias. Visiting his home city briefly from his new residence with his partner David in New York, Tobias had the great fortune of gathering his old friends in one place for a dinner and drinks and long overdue catch up. Samantha immediately felt like she was intruding on this very personal gathering.

Tobias welcomed her with a kiss to both cheeks, as was the French custom and welcomed her to his home with words of familiarity, knowing already so much about Samantha and her travels around Europe, her blogging and her soulmate journey. Tobias couldn't wait to show her into his room and share with her the finished library, an impressive hand-made wooden bookcase that spanned from floor to ceiling, wrapping around two large walls of the room. The king-sized bed in the corner of the room paled in comparison to the massive structure.

He took a moment to stop and grab her by both hands. "You've been crying love." He spoke with compassion and care for his new guest.

"I'm ok," Samantha tried to convince him.

"Here honey, I can fix you." He spoke without waiting for approval and opened a drawer to produce a small black jar. He twisted the lid and dipped his finger inside, he gently dabbed the soothing, cold substance under Samantha's eyes. "This will work magic honey. Just give it a second."

Samantha's tears welled in her eyes once more at the kindness of this stranger.

"Here, here. Don't do that, you will ruin your face already and I don't have enough cream in the house to fix that big of a mess," he smiled as he tried to lighten the mood.

Samantha wrapped her arms around him and thanked him profusely. She kissed him on both cheeks and shared appreciation to the universe for sending her these magical muses, just one after another.

"Do you miss your David when you are apart and here in Paris without him?"

"Yes, I guess, but when I am here I have my lover to keep me company."

"A lover?" Samantha queried him, wondering if she had heard him properly.

"Yes, my dear. A true Parisian man will always take a lover. It is what we do."

"But, what if David found out. What would he say?"

Tobias shook his head. Rarely had he the need to explain the concept of a lover before. He paused to try to think of the correct words in English to explain the long held French tradition of taking a lover.

"David understands my custom. He is a not-so-traditional American, if you can believe there is such a thing. I would have it no other way."

"What does he think of you being with other people?"

"Oh dear, it is not his right to think anything of how I live my life. He knows I love him. I have strong feelings for my lover as well. One does not take away from the other."

Samantha couldn't imagine wanting to be intimate with anyone else but David. She couldn't bear to imagine him wanting to have anyone else besides her as well. She wondered if her traditional values were a result of her own conservative upbringing and if she would have felt differently if she had grown up in Paris.

"So, they both know of the other?"

"Yes, of course." Tobias paused for a moment. "It always surprises me, this traditional view of love that some cultures have. We have enough love in our hearts to share with many people. It is like a parent who loves their first child, they can't imagine ever loving someone more. Then the second child arrives and instantly there is an equal abundance of this overwhelming love for this child as well. Loving one person does not mean we cannot love another at the same time. I love both David and Nathan, just differently. Not one more and the other less. Just differently."

Once they were sorted and ready for the party again, Samantha and Tobias made their way from the bedroom to complete the tour of the generous apartment. Tobias dragged her by the hand through one room after another, sharing his prized fireplace, an apartment centrepiece that during one particularly radical legislative act was threatened to be boarded up as the local council decreed fireplaces to be environmentally damaging. As the government informed their residents that fireplaces could no longer be used, fireplace parties were held across the city as on the final night the city burned white clouds of smoke before their beloved fireplaces were to be taken away. Fortunately, the council reneged and decided that their residents could keep their treasured warm hub of fire within their homes.

As the tour ended and Samantha's glass was nearly finished, Tobias raced Samantha back to the crowded kitchen to fill her glass from the largest champagne bottle she had ever seen. The French surely knew how to live life. These bottles looked double the size she had seen anywhere in her travels and they just kept coming. All night the champagne flowed. Each friend taking turns to refill the glass of their mysterious surprise guest.

Tobias's lover, Nathan shoved a large wooden spoon under Samantha's nose and then graciously placed it into her mouth. In his best English, he enquired as to the taste. It was undoubtedly one of the most exquisite tomato-based sauces Samantha had ever tasted. This was the pizza sauce. It was obvious it had been simmering and sampling for some time as each person was then given another taste of the delicious substance. Some offering ideas of what it needed. Samantha with her limited understanding of the French language understood only small words here and there but was able to make up for it with her instinctual knowledge and skill in reading body language.

Seamus hardly left her side, instead translating those conversations that she needed to know and checking her comfort at being the only foreigner in this close-knit group of friends who had obviously become family. Samantha watched as the pizzas were made with great precision and care. The first one being vegetarian and offered to the new guest. Samantha was impressed and wondered how they knew. It was revealed that during the short timeframe between accepting the invitation and arriving, preparations and shopping had been made to prepare a vegetarian meal for their guest of honour.

Samantha was humbled at the thoughtfulness of her host and overcome with affection for the group. When individuals apologised for speaking French in her presence, knowing she couldn't understand much, if any of the conversation, Samantha fell over herself with gratitude for them. Each time someone was around her they spoke their best English but it wasn't long before the conversation inevitability turned back to French with Samantha having to pick up on odd words to stay involved.

The meal was delicious and the company divine. Samantha wasn't looking forward to the night ending but shouldn't have been worried, as it seemed in Paris, the night is always young. Another spoon, this time a small silver spoon filled to the brim with a clear liquid was forced into her mouth.

"It's gin!" Nathan announced excitedly. And it was the smoothest, most full-bodied gin Samantha had ever had flow down her throat.

"It's boutique gin" Nathan exclaimed until his English restrained him and Seamus explained further that the gin was made from a boutique distiller locally who chooses a different liquor to produce each month. They had all relished the chance to purchase the gin and were saving the exquisite liquid for a special occasion. Tonight, it was as a topping for their freshly cut fruit salad.

Fruit salad with a twist, the taste was to die for. The left-over gin was to replenish the thirsty crowd but only after Seamus, the passionate barman made Samantha depart and find fresh lemons and tonic to finish off the perfect gin and tonic. As they exited the lush apartment into the cold, both more than slightly inebriated, Samantha felt such comfort as Seamus once again in his role of protector made sure the night time traffic slowed as they crossed the street. The comfort they shared being in each other's presence felt so very natural.

Upon returning and embarking on the huge spiral staircase once more, Tobias, Nathan, Seamus and Samantha enjoyed some quiet gin and tonics. The crowd had dispersed and Samantha wondered if it was time for her too to leave and allow the friends to catch up long into the morning. Nathan asked again, "So how do you two know each other?"

Samantha laughed as she suggested Seamus was her paid tour guide, joining her as part of his contractual arrangements when she rented out the apartment. Seamus looked displeased as he whispered to her, "I hope you don't think this is what this is."

Samantha felt horrible. There was nothing she wanted to do to upset her new friend, especially after how wonderfully gracious and inviting he had been of her bringing her along for this special gathering. One final drink and the boutique gin was finished. Onto a new and hopefully equally exquisite liquor next month.

Samantha bid her farewells, somewhat sad to have to say goodbye to these wonderful people to journey back to her quiet apartment all alone for the night. Seamus walked Samantha downstairs ready to hop on his bike himself. As he did he asked her if she wanted a walk home, Samantha was all too pleased to accept. After all that champagne and gin, she was feeling a little less confident on finding her way back to her lovely little apartment.

Walking back, they talked about David, and Samantha's fear that she may never see him again. It had been weeks already and although she completely understood and felt for what David was going through, part of her didn't understand why she couldn't go to him. She missed him immensely and imagined he felt the same but found it all hard to understand.

"Do you want to come up for a scotch?" Samantha asked Seamus.

"Of course, I thought you would never ask," he responded with enthusiasm. Once upstairs Seamus readjusted the heating as if it was his own home. He felt more than comfortable in the apartment having visited it many times before to hand over keys for his friend.

The duo found some music, keeping it soft given the time of the night, they then decided to find a warm spot on the couch to chat.

As was becoming the norm for them, the conversation flowed freely. They covered off on the normal topics of family, travel and philosophy and added a new topic around spirits and the afterlife into the conversation. As it turned out, the apartment they had just visited had been the scene for a horrific death of a young man, and his spirit it seemed had visited Seamus more than once when he was there. Both friends were in agreement that after death, the spirit remained, neither knew where, but it was without question for them both that the spirit lived on and was somehow able to communicate with the living. Both agreed they felt some comfort in the knowledge that they would live on and reassured even more to know that loved ones were always looking over them.

"What was the message you had from the young man who died there?" Samantha asked.

"Not so much a message, but a feeling. A deeply penetrating feeling of great pain and misery. A feeling so strong that to go on living wasn't an option."

"How did he die?"

"He was found hung in the main lounge."

Samantha caught the lump in her throat. The tears welled in her eyes.

"Samantha?" Seamus enquired softly as he leaned into her. "Are you ok?"

"That is how my sister killed herself."

Seamus wrapped his arms around her. I am so sorry darling. Please let us change the subject. Let's talk about what our little gang banging tourist friend must be up to tonight.

The memory made Samantha smile.

"It's ok. It is probably time I talked about her. It has been years I have avoided it."

Seamus sat back, fixed the blanket back over them both and waited for Samantha to talk.

"Sarah killed herself straight after we buried our father. We had no clue, not even a hint that it was something she had ever contemplated."

"That to me indicates a person with their mind made up. Why do you think she did it?"

"She missed Dad. We both did. It wasn't that either one of us were closer to him than the other. It is just that… I don't know, I really don't have any idea why. That is what hurts the most to be left living with the not knowing. No note, no discussion, no good-byes."

Seamus was thoughtful and sensitive as he offered up some form of understanding, "If she was feeling anything like the young man in the apartment, there might not have been much thought to it, not much exploration of how and when things would feel better. I get the sense from the young man, that death was the only way he knew to make the great pain he felt disappear. If that makes sense."

"I think so."

"For what I have come to understand after giving it much thought. The pain of living was greater than the pain of dying."

"Why didn't she understand that the pain of death, the grieving it never goes away but it does get easier?"

"That my dear, is because you allowed yourself to work through the grief. With time you have begun to heal the loss of your father. I don't know your sister, but I know you have a great deal of resilience within you. I hear that in the stories you share. In the adventures you embark on. Maybe you had a strength that your sister didn't."

Samantha paused as she reflected on the wise words of her friend.

"I'm not sure about that. I think I would describe it more as a loyalty. A loyalty and a promise to my father to live the best life I could."

"And have you?" Seamus challenged.

"I think I am starting to. Being here, meeting you. Meeting David, that has been the start of something that I know my father would have wanted for me. Up until now I had felt kind of paralyzed, frozen in grief. Unable to take the next step, and then suddenly I felt this urge, this instinct to fly directly to Rome."

"And there you met your soulmate," Seamus added.

"And there I met my soulmate," Samantha agreed.

Seamus had more to ask, "What do you think that instinct was? Could it have been your father or sister somehow telling you to make the trip?"

Samantha smiled. "If they could do that and lead me to David, do you think they could also send me some lottery numbers?"

The friends laughed, Seamus picked up Samantha's scotch and placed it in her hand. They clicked the glasses together as Seamus made the toast: "To instincts, messages from our loved ones, to trusting yourself and following the right path."

"And to soulmates," Samantha added as they clicked their glasses in unison once more.

Once again the conversation turned to love and soulmates. Samantha felt less and less sure each day about her future with David. As much as she knew he was her soulmate, she couldn't maintain a strong faith that he would return to her. It was as if each time they met briefly they would connect with such intensity but that connection wasn't to be sustained.

Maybe this was due to the immense passion and strength of their soulmate connection or maybe Samantha just couldn't be sure of anything anymore. The champagne and gin were now taking their toll and Samantha started to feel tired. The two friends sat closely on the couch chatting away. It was just the comfort she needed. She let her head drop and rest on Seamus's shoulder.

"I'm glad we are friends," Samantha blurted out.

Seamus repositioned himself to look directly at her. "If I am being honest Samantha, this feels like more than friendship to me." And with that declaration, he wasted no time and leaned forward to kiss her.

Before Samantha could comprehend what was happening, his lips were on hers. For a moment, she allowed the warmth and passion to continue until she pulled away devastated at what she had allowed to happen.

"Seamus, I can't do that… David…" she shared.

Seamus was unapologetic for his actions, instead insisting that there is more than one soulmate for every person. "I know Samantha. I know you think you love David, but you feel something for me too. And I you!" He implored her for understanding.

This was no drunken mistake. Seamus had begun to realise his feelings for Samantha and felt no remorse in acting on them.

"Let's go to bed," Seamus suggested. "We can talk more in the morning, nothing will happen, we are both tired. Let's just get some sleep."

Samantha woke in the morning and Seamus was already busy in the kitchen brewing coffee. The aroma of the fragrant bean filled the apartment. They took their coffee outside and talked more about soulmates and love and destiny and life after death. Samantha began to cough, a cough that was persistent but much worse at some times than others.

"Maybe you need to see someone about that. I can take you to a doctor today if you want," he suggested, concerned for his friend. This cold weather was nothing like she was used to and he didn't want to see her become unwell, not when things were just taking off with her blogging again.

"No, it's nothing at all. I just have this cough thing," Samantha insisted. He walked inside to grab an extra blanket and wrap it around her shoulders.

"I just want to keep you well my friend," he assured her.

Ten

The Louvre, Paris

Before Samantha could leave the enchanting city of Paris, she had one more place she absolutely needed to see. She walked through the quiet morning streets to the impressive structure that housed within it, some of the greatest artistic treasures from history. The Louvre was the home of Venus de Milo, the ancient Greek sculpture of Aphrodite as well as, what is said to be the most famous artwork of all, the impressive Mona Lisa.

Samantha took her time, taking in every glorious piece the magnificent building housed. She paused frequently to focus her camera, catching the rays of light that shone through the glass doors framing the artwork with hues of orange. Stopping only for a quick bite to eat, Samantha flitted away the entire day exploring the various levels and massive rooms of the museum.

Taking the escalator back up to the main street at the end of the day, the crowded Parisian city was alive before her once more. A middle aged man standing beside her on the ascent to street level uttered a few words in French to her. Samantha had barely noticed the man standing beside her and wondered for a second who he was speaking to before she realised he was addressing the conversation to her.

"Oh, I am sorry. I speak only a little bit of French," Samantha informed him.

"Excuse me," the man replied. "I thought you were a French local."

Samantha smiled at the notion. She would have very much loved to have lived in this city. The ride to the top was complete and

Samantha walked from the escalator to head to the busy city centre. The man beside her continued to talk.

"Where are you from?"

"Australia."

"And you travel in Paris alone?"

"Yes, well I am meeting my partner when he can join me, but for the meantime I am alone."

"Well, you must join me for a glass of wine. Come, we can go to the bar just across the road here."

Samantha had no reason to reject the surprise request. Experience on her travels to date had shown her that sometimes the most unexpected and pleasant encounters occurred with the meeting of two absolute strangers.

The duo dodged the traffic to enter the cosy wine bar. They found a seat near the window and began their introductions.

"I'm Frederic," the stranger announced as he presented his hand to shake.

"I'm Samantha. I'm travelling for a while as I create blogs of my adventures."

"A writer? Let me read some of your words?"

Samantha clumsily searched for her phone in her bag and found her website quickly. She handed her new friend the phone and sat back to await his comments. The wine waiter approached and without looking up Frederic ordered deux vin blanc. Samantha knew enough French to understand that to mean two white wines.

"Oh la la!" Frederic exclaimed, his eyes not leaving the screen.

Samantha sat silently. The wines arrived and she took a large gulp. The experience itself feeling quite surreal. She looked around the room. Happy couples shared a pre-dinner cocktail or an after-work drink. The cosy little bar was warm and inviting. The wait staff, in no rush laughed with one another as they stood surrounding the bar area. As she glanced outside the window, she noticed the beginnings of a soft rain. It accentuated the ambiance of the romantic setting.

Finally, Frederic lifted his head from the phone screen and handed the mobile back to Samantha. He seized his wine glass and raised it in a toast.

"To muses." He clicked his glass against Samantha's.

Samantha couldn't agree more and what a lovely coincidence to hear the word, muses, again while in Paris. It was a curious notion to hear repeated. It was as if Paris itself acknowledged the mystical and divine magical power of the creative muse.

"What do you do Frederic?"

"I write also. I write for The Louvre."

Samantha was impressed. "Can I see some of your work?"

Frederic reached over and took Samantha's phone once more. He found The Louvre website and directed her to a page on the magnificent works. His writing was unimaginably complex and divinely musical in a way. The words teased and flirted with each other, striking at emotions, pulling the reader from their reality and into the world of the gorgeous artwork they were describing.

"Oh la la!" Samantha exclaimed, "You are very talented."

"Merci," Frederic replied.

"Do you have any feedback for me? Any words to help me improve my writing?"

"Your writing is your savoir faire, oui?"

Samantha was puzzled. Although she had heard the word savior faire before, she wasn't sure how it pertained to her writing.

"Please explain."

"The French describe a person's grace or talent as their savoir faire. I can already see some of yours. Your savoir faire is your beauty, your smile, your talent for words and your sense of adventure."

"And yours?"

"Mine is love and my writing. You like the wine?"

"Oui."

Frederic raised his hand to gesture to the waiter for two more glasses. There was a privileged air to his movements. A sense of belonging in the world, of knowing his place with no apologies for doing so. Samantha enjoyed the company of this self-assured Parisian.

"How do you write with such emotion. It is as if I can taste your words, your words evoke every sense in the reader. How do you do this?"

"The French have a complex and rich history. We are a proud people, sophisticated one might say in a way that others are not."

"Go on."

"Those born here are both conservative and free thinking. We appreciate the ways in which we like to live, we live by simple unspoken rules. We cherish the arts and connection with our rich history. Take for example our language."

"Yes, not an easy one to learn."

"But beautiful, oui?"

"Yes, extremely, listening to the French spoken language is like what I would imagine it to feel to have a smooth, rich honey poured over sensitive skin.

"A very enticing image, any French man would appreciate. Our language is fiercely protected. No word is permitted to enter our dictionaries without careful and passionate debate over its appropriateness for inclusion. We have an entire department dedicated to this very task. We do not deviate from our language just because a new term or popular word has infiltrated other countries' dialects. We stay true to our rich history and culture."

"This rigidity has then created a purity of language. It is a beautiful thing."

"Beauty is what the French are known for."

"I think the Romans may debate that with you?" Samantha challenged him.

"And they would be mistaken."

Frederic followed Samantha out onto the street. He reached for the lapels of her thick winter coat and pulled them together. He reached forward and fastened the buttons on the front of her coat in a protective gesture designed to keep her warm.

"I would like you to be my lover. Only my lover and no one else's."

"I have a partner. I told you that already."

"This doesn't matter. I have a partner too."

"No," Samantha was forceful in her reply. "I understand and respect your tradition, but it is not mine."

Frederic kissed her gently on the cheek.

"If you change your mind, here is my number. I live not far from here and work each day at The Louvre. I can make arrangements if you call."

Samantha took the card and re-stated her rejection of the offer. As surprising as it was to be propositioned in such a way, it was a unique experience to witness first-hand how simple it is in Paris to take a lover. This was definitely an exploit her blog readers would be keen to hear about. Samantha was now excited and energised to go back to the little apartment and write some more.

After another week in Paris, Samantha was ready to explore somewhere new and had more than enough material to write her Paris blog. She boarded the fast train to Berlin and prepared to type. The words came quickly and with ease. She had so much inspiration from her time in Paris that she knew exactly the theme for her page.

***

Blog Post – Paris

Paris… the City of Love
Paris, Paris… what can I say about Paris… the city that leaves her scent on your skin, your lips and your fingertips. She agitates you with desire, her power over confusing the succession of your thoughts. If Rome was the city of beauty, Paris must be the city of passion.

As I rented a gorgeous little apartment in the second district, I told my landlord it was to continue to write my blogs on her terrace. She had inspired me with her generosity of spirit. She was a deeply creative soul and with the magical powers of the arts she wished for me a muse, a muse, to help me to create my very own fictional story of love.

And they came. With powers so strong, she conjured up not one, but many beautiful, creative, inspiring muses… photographers, writers, musicians, composers, singers and art history aficionados.

With these heady mix of characters at play, I soon envisaged myself, the poor impoverished writer, calling Paris home for a while. I wanted to soak up every ounce of their creativity. I wanted to live in their world, see what they see, share their emotional turmoil of the city that breathes passion.

Hours and hours talking with a very talented photographer with a brilliant mind about art, science, physics, philosophy, psychology, religion, family and home. He allowed me into his world for a short time meeting his eclectic groups of friends, now his family.

I felt embraced into their home, welcomed into their world as the insane Aussie travelling through Europe. The muses continued, the singer/composer/musician who loves artwork and found inspiration for music in the galleries and museums of Paris.

A fellow writer, a soulmate of sorts writing in her head all day, walking the streets with a smile as she conjures up the next sexy storyline of her plot. Living with her characters day and night as if they were friends she had always known.

The art history aficionado working so closely with the priceless treasures that surround him, knowing every inch of them in a way that the rest of us could only dream. Inspired by their beauty, richness and history he exuberated passion from every pore. His profound words ignite every sense in the body.

These were my muses. Each with their own savoir faire, so used to living with such greatness, the French have their very own word for it. Their savoir faire... for each it was different... culture, nature, anticipating, whispering words, writing, feeling, learning, touching, inspiring, being born to love, kissing... and yes, the Parisians love their kissing and speak of it often. These were their talents, their passions. I am sure there were many more hidden treasures they were too proud to assign.

My muses grant me my own savior-faire... charm, writing, imagination, perception and beauty. I accept them graciously. And as I feel more and more a part of their world, I start to question the notion of home. We chat about it, what makes a home, what is home, is it a place or a feeling? For one, it was friends, for another it was the culture of their home city of Paris, the place they were born. For another it was their family home, maybe a distant memory but the home they grew up in nevertheless. I am reminded time and time again that I live in one of the most beautiful natural countries in the world, a country that many could only wish to know.

I begin to wonder if I could one day call this city of passion home. As I write this last sentence on a train in the South of France, saying goodbye to this beautiful country, for now a mass of glistening blue water opens up before me beckoning me to stay basking in her glory. She is urging me to return.

So, my advice, and I'm not one to normally give advice, but you really should experience Paris, the home of parties of consumption and debauchery. And I jest with the city a little as I say that, but we all do know there is always some small element of truth to every legend.

If you come to Paris, don't listen to those who might say that the Parisians are rude people, that they won't speak English to you even though they can. Sure, see the sights, The Eiffel Tower, the Arc de Triomphe, Notre Dame, Champs Elysees, Moulin Rouge, the Palais Garnier and especially, The Louvre.

But please also meet the locals, the native born, the expats, the passionate blend of creative individuals who choose to call Paris home. Find your own savoir faire… learn theirs! And for those of you who might need their very own muse, let me know. I might try and see if some of their magical wonderment can be shared amongst friends.

Rome, you certainly taught me to appreciate beauty and a little of my heart remains with you but Paris you have left me undeniably changed forever. The passion that you have generously shared with me will inspire me always. I leave with you my beautiful muses. Take good care of them until I see them again.

Eleven

Los Angeles, California

David made another coffee, one for him and one for his little brother. The two men sat at their family dining table to have a much needed and long overdue conversation about their father.

Caleb was the first to speak. "David, we need to get Dad to speak to someone. He isn't improving."

David couldn't have agreed more but now having sampled the love that his father spoke of, he understood more deeply than ever the pain he was going through.

"He needs time. This is going to just take time," David tried to reassure his brother.

"We don't have time, neither of us do. We both have lives we need to get back to," Caleb made a passionate plea to his brother.

David agreed but letting the words escape his lips would only make him think of Samantha. His mind wandered immediately to his soulmate. He wished he knew what she was doing this very second. Was she thinking of him too? He closed his eyes as the pain of their separation caused an ache in his chest. He knew he had been distanced from her by land, but also the distance he had created emotionally from her in order to be present for his family, his face seared thinking of the pain he had caused her.

Caleb sensed he wasn't going to get much debate from his brother and continued with his argument of logic. "David, I have business meetings I need to attend. I can't keep putting people off." He paused knowing all too well that David too had pressing issues that he needed to see to, not the least of all his new-found relationship. "David, I know you need to get back to Samantha. If I have learnt nothing more from this senseless experience, it is that you can't ignore love when it finds you."

David nodded silently in agreement.

"What are we going to do?" Caleb continued, pressing for a joint decision about the future care of their much-loved father.

David couldn't bear to be away from Samantha any longer, but he couldn't leave his father just yet either. He was torn between the man who raised him, the loving parent who had just lost the woman he spent his entire life loving and David's own soulmate, his Samantha, who he wanted to join to begin his own journey with.

He finally spoke, "Caleb, you go and take care of what you need to. I will stay with Dad for a while longer."

Caleb was enthused by the release from his familial responsibilities. He needed to ensure his business was running smoothly in order to be in a position to take care of his father should his grieving become more complex. He was reluctant to leave but knew that the sooner he could tie up loose ends, the sooner he could be back in the family home and allow David some much needed time away.

David went to check on his father, taking a tea for comfort. He sat down beside his father's bed and tried to rouse him.

"Dad, how are you feeling?" he began.

His father opened his eyes slightly, blinking as if the light from the window offended the very sense it sought to nourish. He wanted to be strong but he had lost his will to fight it anymore. Seeing his son, beside him now, the man that he himself used to be, he struggled to sit up to greet him.

David continued, gently urging his father to find his strength once more.

"Dad, here is a tea for you." He watched as the older man took it, sipping it immediately. He watched the comforting liquid warm his throat.

His father looked straight into his eyes. "Why are you still here son?"

"I can't be anywhere else right now Dad. Not until you are feeling better."

"What about your lady love?" his father asked. Trying desperately to remember her name in his sleepy haze, his father was apologetic. "I'm sorry son, I can't seem, to remember her name."

"It's ok Dad, it's Samantha. And she is fine. Actually Dad, there is something I wanted to tell you about Samantha."

"Yes, son, what is it?"

"You have met her before."

"How? Where?"

"A long time ago. Do you remember the holiday we took to Fiji? You, me, mum and Caleb?"

"Yes, of course. Your mother loved the country. The people always welcoming us all day long with their greeting of Bula. And Fiji time. She had to try to contain her impatience when people worked on Fiji time. It was as if they rejected clocks. Things just happened when they happened. There was no rushing them."

The men stopped and smiled together of the memory of their family holiday.

"Dad, do you remember how all the parents seemed to connect and the kids just kinda ran wild across the island, swimming, learning how the locals climbed coconut trees. Eating coconut all day."

"Oh, I do hope you didn't feel as if your mother and I neglected you. It just seemed you and Caleb were having so much fun with your little friends."

"We did. Do you remember the twin girls from Australia?"

"Oh yes, they were a couple of cuties. You boys spent a lot of time with those girls. What were their names again?"

"Samantha and Sarah," David replied.

"Yes, yes that's right. Their parents were lovely too, we had many a dinner with them."

David let his father reminisce before he spoke moments later.

"Dad, that Samantha is my Samantha."

His father looked at him in shock. "But how can that be?"

"I have no answer. Fate, the universe, some divine force of nature. She travelled to Rome and walked straight into my tour group."

"Oh dear, who would have thought that even possible. But how did you know it was her? After all those years, how did you recognise her again?"

"A man always remembers his first kiss Dad. It was just an innocent peck between kids, but she captured my heart."

His father's tears gathered in his eyes. "Just like your mother was my first kiss."

The men enjoyed a meaningful silence. An unspoken connection of understanding was formed between them.

"Son, I want to meet her again. I want to meet the woman you will marry. Where is she?"

"She understands I need to be here for a while. She is travelling."

"Travelling, with whom?"

"Alone, Dad, she is a blogger and is travelling alone through Europe for inspiration. She is fine, she is a strong woman and I will join her when I can."

"No son!" His father struggled to his feet. "No son, you can't let the woman you love, travel alone. Do you know the trouble a woman alone can get into?"

"Dad, sit and relax. It's ok. She is ok. She does this all the time. She can take care of herself."

His father's anger was obvious now. "How can a son of mine, say that to me? She is your responsibility. You need to look after her. She shouldn't have to take care of herself. That is your job. Is this how I have raised you son?"

David felt ashamed beyond words. He knew that his father wasn't in the frame of mind to squabble with. He realised that much of his argument came from the guilt he still felt at the loss of the woman he loved for nearly four decades. He wondered how long he would blame himself for a terrible accident that no one could have foreseen. David ached to see his father in this much pain. He had no idea how to help him. For the first time in his life he felt absolutely helpless. No words could take away the pain or bring his mother back. No second-guessing could help anyone feel differently about the loss of a great woman, wife and mother.

"Dad, sit down please," David begged of him.

"I will not! I am still your father and you will do as I say." His father stood tall for the first time since his mother's accident.

"Ok Dad, I will. Please just relax, sit. Let's just talk, finish your tea and let's talk about it."

"Don't tell me what to do. I am not a feeble, old man. I am your father and you need to hear what I have to say…" His father clutched at his chest, his opened palm grabbing the muscle in his left chest. His face turned red, he gasped for breath. David reached up to grab him just as his father fell into his arms.

David dropped to the floor, holding his father tightly in his embrace. He called through the house to his brother, "Caleb! Caleb! Come quickly! Call an ambulance!"

Caleb ran into the room, his phone in his hand. He reached down for his father as David yelled to him, "Call an ambulance! I think Dad has had a heart attack."

The boys placed their father's limp body on the bedroom floor and checked his breathing and pulse. They began immediately to assist him to breathe. Taking turns until the ambulance arrived to administer breaths and chest compressions in a vain attempt to restart his heart.

When the ambulance arrived, they worked for another twenty minutes but to no avail. Their father had passed. The sons had kept a bedside vigil for their devastated father, but in the end, he died of a broken heart. There was nothing they could do to save him.

* * *

The men unable to grasp the enormity of their loss settled for a small service with immediate family and friends. There were no eulogies from David or Caleb. There were simply no words left to be said. Friends tried to speak to the brothers about a sense of fulfillment that their parents were together once more. Some suggesting their father's loss was inevitable given the cause of his grief and great suffering. The brothers instead chose to remain tight lipped. There was nothing that could explain away their anguish at the loss of both of their beloved parents in such a short space of time.

David's mind, when it could, returned to thoughts of Samantha, his cherished soulmate. He knew he had neglected her for far too long but felt it wasn't fair to burden her with his grief. He had of course let her know of his father's passing and as he suspected, she had wanted to rush to be by his side. He needed time alone. He needed to process in whatever way he could the sense of emptiness in his heart.

Time, he just needed more time.

Twelve

Berlin, Germany

Samantha arrived in frosty Berlin to the warm welcome of her university friend, Sedgwick. Thanks to the convenience of social media, Sedgwick had found Samantha again after a long absence in each other's lives. Like Samantha had hoped to one day be, Sedgwick was a world citizen, travelling mainly for work and seeking out friends along the way to make the lonely nights at strange hotels and empty restaurant tables a little more bearable.

Tonight, Sedgwick was entertaining clients at the Brauhouse. A must-do destination on the tourist road trip and a favourite among locals and adventurers alike. Samantha entered the massive beer hall to the sounds of a lively band playing local dance music. The atmosphere forced a smile on her weary face. There was no choice but to be joyful with the jocularity and laughter that abounded in the huge structure. Sedgwick was quick to find Samantha, having been waiting eagerly for hours to catch up with his old friend.

"Hello darling!" he squealed with delight as he wrapped his massive arms around her. He towered over the delicate Samantha and squeezed her, holding her tightly in his embrace. "You feel like skin and bones my dear. What has happened to you?"

Samantha hesitated slightly. She had thought she had lost some weight. Having bought new, smaller jeans in Paris, she imagined the travel and the concern for David had taken a bit of a toll of her already slender frame.

"I've been busy, that's all." She didn't want to raise any further concern for Sedgwick. She knew he had a flair for the dramatic and she didn't want to make her health or any issue for that matter a point of focus for his interrogative tendencies.

"Tell me about you," she tried to change the subject quickly. "How long are you in Berlin for?" She had to speak loudly over the pounding instruments and cheers from the boisterous crowd.

"I'm here for just two days. Have to wine and dine some new clients. You know how it is. Work, work, work," he explained.

She didn't quite know how it was but smiled politely anyway. Sedgwick's career had always been a bit of a mystery to her. He had tried to explain it a number of times before, but Samantha couldn't quite grasp it. She knew he travelled worldwide and enjoyed meals and drinks with clients endlessly but for what reason remained unclear. Nevertheless, he appeared to be doing well for himself and was rarely without a smile these days so she wished him the best of luck in whatever it was he was doing.

"You must have a stein. I will get one for you right away. Oh, and a shot. We must do shots!" He turned to the table of middle-aged men that accompanied him and shouted back his plan. "Shots everyone!" Without a seconds further delay he was off to grab the attention of the busy waiter, hands already full of the oversized beer mugs on his way to service a table. She watched Sedgwick with his wild hand gestures and fingers raised to confirm the number of drinks required as he placed his order. He smiled delightedly as he rushed back to Samantha's side.

"So, tell me quickly. What is happening with this soulmate of yours? Where is he? Is he coming tonight? When do I get to meet him?" The questions were thick and fast and Samantha realised in the craziness of the last couple of days she hadn't yet informed Sedgwick of the traumatic loss of David's father.

"Can we not talk about him right now. I will tell you later," she pleaded with him.

"Ok, ok. But you better spill all later." He let her off the hook for the time being but there was no doubt they would be having a conversation in the very near future, hopefully in a more private setting.

Samantha watched Sedgwick return to his group of overly spirited friends. He strutted to the table, giving a quick squeeze to the bottom of the friend on the left. Then just as quickly and covertly doing the same to his friend on the right. This companion enjoyed the affection so much he immediately returned the favour with a grab of Sedgwick's bottom. Unsure if this was some sort of cultural display of affection, Samantha wasn't sure what to make of it.

She glanced around the room to see if she would see the same pattern of behaviour replicated amongst the densely populated room of mostly European-looking decent. She watched with interest at the comings and goings around her. Loud groups of tables feasted on plates of food large enough to feed an entire family. Beer steins flowed, being emptied as quickly as they could be replenished. Quite obviously tour groups, brought to this famous beer hall to partake of some traditional German culture.

Further into the distance and toward the outskirts of the room, away from the madness of the seven-piece band were the smaller groups, possibly locals, some couples, individual travellers perhaps wanting to come and witness for themselves what all the reviews raved about. And the locals, the locals bringing friends from near and far to celebrate their special occasions. To join the group sing-a-long, the dancing and the conga lines.

Samantha failed to see the now regular bottom squeezing at any other table besides the one frequented by Sedgwick. She wondered if it was perhaps code for something. Maybe, she thought to herself, Sedgwick was a major cocaine dealer and the gesture was the secret signal that a purchase was required. The more Samantha thought about it and the more the alcohol took its effect, the more outrageous her fantasies about Sedgwick had become.

She thought she should try it out for herself. She marched the few steps back to the table, massive stein in one hand, walked straight up to Sedgwick and squeezed his butt cheek.

He turned around immediately to face her. He laughed when he saw her standing beside him waiting for a required response. "Oh honey," Sedgwick laughed as he let the words flow freely, "You can't afford what you are touching."

"What?" Samantha blurted out as an automatic response to Sedgwick's intriguing comment.

Sedgwick turned around to the group, did a quick count of the number of near empty steins, grabbed Samantha by the hand and ushered her to the bar. "Down the rest of that drink, girl. You have been nursing it for days." When close enough he motioned to the server behind the bar, the number of steins required. Finally, all business concluded, he turned back to Samantha.

She was smiling and had just one important question to ask of her friend. "Sedgey, baby, are you an escort?" she giggled at the thought of it.

"Corporate companion my dear. I am far more valuable than any ordinary escort. Those men, they might take to dinner my dear. I offer a much more extensive service."

"Do tell…" Samantha was keen to hear more from her entrepreneurial-minded friend.

Sedgwick did not hold back. He explained the overarching concept behind his seemingly successful business venture.

"I am both their business advisor and lover in one perfect package. I travel with them, I introduce them to people they would otherwise not meet and I bring them pleasure when they would otherwise be alone in an empty hotel room."

"Are these men married?" Samantha wanted to ask the question, not sure she would be ready for the answer.

"Most," was her friend's vague response to the very personal question.

"Most?" She was in too far now and needed to know more.

"Yes, most are married men. That is not for you or I to judge, so get that look off your precious little face."

Sedgwick paused for a moment. He took Samantha's hands in his and looked in the face of his naïve friend. "My dear, all men are gay deep down in their soul." He let go of her hands, throwing them into the air for dramatic effect. "It is just the way it is. Why deny ourselves what we really want? Life is too short."

The questions forming in Samantha's head now were accumulating quickly. "Ok, ok, so even if that is true... How does this all work? Do you sleep with all of them?"

Sedgwick laughed. "Not even I am that good, my dear. No, tonight is a little tricky, two of the men are previous clients but only one has booked me for the stay."

"What will you do?"

"I guess I will just give the other a quick blowie in the bathroom. That should appease him until I see him again."

Samantha raised her hand to her mouth. Her eyes widened at the thought of what her friend was about to do.

"Now, don't you dare be so judgey with me, my dear. I knew you back as a young thing in university. I could tell a story or two about you as well you know."

Samantha nodded her head in acceptance. She didn't for a moment hold any judgement for the business that Sedgwick was undertaking. It was a different thought that was going through her mind that raised concern for her.

"No, it's just you kissed me on the lips when I arrived." She smiled to indicate her humour in the situation. "Who knows where your mouth has already been tonight."

The friends laughed and Sedgwick gave Samantha a huge squeeze. He knew of all people Samantha would be one to not judge his money-making venture. The pair watched as the refills of their beers were taken to their nearby table.

The massive stein of amber liquid went straight to her head. The lack of food on the train trip and the headiness of the busy atmosphere, made her start to spin. The free-flowing shots probably didn't help her predicament.

"Sedgwick," she yelled above the crowd, "I think I need some fresh air."

"Ok," he replied, far too caught up in entertaining his posse to deter her from leaving.

Samantha pushed her way through the energetic crowd, barely escaping the desperate grasps of an overweight, sweating, bearded man in long socks as he reached to pull her into the expanding conga line. She smiled politely into the steely eyes of the security guard on position at the entrance in the hope that he might let her queue jump the impressive crowd waiting for free table space to be allowed entry.

Samantha stepped outside and instantly the noise of the band eased away as the tiny white snowflakes began landing on her long black sleeves.

"Snow!" she exclaimed excitedly. This was the first snow Samantha had encountered in her current travels. "Snow!" she cried out again to no-one in particular. She raised her palms to the sky in a vain attempt to capture the icy particles of glistening beauty falling from the sky. For a moment, Samantha's worries were forgotten as she spun around in the falling snow, arms outstretched as she took in the beauty of the light white snowfall surrounding her.

* * *

David looked at his phone once more, checking the time in Berlin, he was curious about what Samantha might be doing at that exact moment. He figured it would be around twelve-thirty where she was, just after midnight. He hoped she was enjoying herself. He wanted so desperately to be with her and he wondered for a moment if she might still be awake. He picked up his phone and on a spur-of-the-moment decision rang her number.

* * *

The ringing of her phone in her jeans pocket shocked Samantha back into reality. She lowered her arms, stood still and reefed the phone from the denim.

"Hello?" she smiled as she answered, not bothering to look at the number but happy to chat with whomever may be ringing.

"Hello beautiful," David's deep mellow voice immediately warmed her soul as her cheeks flushed at the sound.

"Hello." She was surprised to hear from him.

The sweet tones of that one word was enough to melt David's heart completely. He felt tears well of joy as he visualised her gorgeous face smiling down at him through the phone.

"I miss you more than you could imagine." He spoke softly as he made the declaration.

"I miss you too." Her tone more void of emotion. The alcohol still affecting her ability to connect the voice with the overwhelming relief at hearing from him. In a more-sober state, Samantha herself would most likely be weeping down the phone to the man she missed so very much.

"Do you still love me?" he teased her gently.

"To the moon and back," she playfully promised him.

"And I love you more than you could ever imagine." He paused as he recognised instantly what he had to say next, "Would you like a visitor?"

"Yes, oh yes!" she screamed

"Where in the world will I find you in a couple of days?" he questioned her, although he had a fairly good idea she would be staying in Germany for a while longer yet.

"Berlin for a few more days at least… I can wait here for you," she hinted with reservation, not quite knowing how long before she would see her beloved David again.

He was quick to respond. He couldn't wait a second longer to be with her. "I'm on the next plane, beautiful. See you soon."

She ended the call and screamed with joy as she jumped in the air. The combination of the slippery ice-ridden sidewalk and the copious shots resulted in her landing with a heavy thud on the cold surface. At that exact moment Sedgwick appeared on the street behind her, wasting no time in pulling out his phone to capture the epic fail of a moment. Several onlookers laughed, two ran over to her side to assist her back to her feet. Samantha couldn't have cared less. She roared with laughter at her own clumsiness and screamed at Sedgwick when she noticed him behind her.

"He's coming to Berlin!" she yelled at him. "He's coming to Berlin!"

"Well about time," was all Sedgwick had to offer. Samantha's excitement at the news of her lover's arrival did little to reassure Sedgwick of the already long list of concerns he had about the man he hoped to soon meet.

Thirteen

Berlin, Germany

Samantha looked at the plate in front of her. "Is there anything else to eat in Germany besides meat?"

Sedgwick laughed. "Fortunately for me meat is their preferred food of choice. The bratwurst, rostbratwurst, bockwurst, bregenwurst, knackwurst, landjager and let's not forget the faithful old leberwurst. Strangely enough all sausages come to think of it. The Germans do like their sausages." He smirked at his own crudeness. "Eat up. It will help with your hangover," he encouraged his friend.

"I think I am going to be sick," Samantha confessed, turning green at the sight of the plate full of animal carcass in front of her.

"Either way, you will probably throw up. Just eat something to soak up the alcohol."

"Can I just go to sleep please?" Samantha begged her friend. The night continued much longer than Samantha had intended and here they were early morning consuming what looked to Samantha to be a plate of greasy sausages, an egg and a piece of bread. "I can't eat this. I will be sick. I need sleep."

The extraordinary news that David was coming to meet Samantha in Berlin had meant that celebrations had been in order. Once back at the table at the Brauhouse the old friends joined Sedgwick's work associates for more beers, more shots of anything alcoholic and hours upon hours of dancing and singing. Sedgwick still wasn't convinced that this new man in Samantha's life was worth all the fuss and he had every intention of finding out more before he arrived.

"Samantha, tell me more about this David of yours?" Sedgwick began his line of questioning.

Samantha looked up from her untouched breakfast. "I can tell already from the way you asked that question, that you don't approve."

"I wouldn't say I don't approve. It is just that this all happened very suddenly my dear and then he just vanishes on you."

Samantha understood that she still hadn't filled Sedgwick in on the tragic death of David's father. She told him the devasting details of David's father's sudden heart attack. Of both sons being there and not being able to save him. Of the small funeral that was so sad neither man could stand up to pay tribute to their father. Samantha had tears flowing as she shared how worried she was about David and how heartbroken he was at losing both parents so quickly and without reason.

Sedgwick was thoughtful as he listened to the overwhelming news. He could see how invested Samantha was with this new love. She shared in his pain. He could tell that she wanted nothing more than to see him again. He made sure he put the next few words to her gently.

"Sam, I just wonder if you might be trying to fill a void?"

Samantha felt instantly sober but still extremely hung-over and nauseous. She knew exactly what Sedgwick meant by his statement.

She shook her head in disagreement. "Not at all. One, has nothing to do with the other."

"One what Samantha?" Sedgwick knew he had touched on something and thought it was about time Samantha stopped running away from her problems.

"What are you asking me, Sedgwick?" Samantha did not want to continue this conversation. She had more than a good idea about where it was heading.

"You have not even uttered her name to me once since she died. I don't think you have faced your own grief and I think this David is just an elaborate cover up to not feel the pain anymore."

He had said it. He had said the exact thought that had been ruminating through his mind since he had heard about the sad death of Samantha's twin sister.

"You want me to tell you I miss Sarah?" Samantha paused.

Saying her sister's name out loud was more difficult than she imagined it would be. "Of course, I miss her. I miss her every day. I just want to be able to speak to her again. To tell her everything that she has missed. To tell her..." Her voice trailed out. She was finally saying the words she had longed to say but it was to the wrong person. She wanted to be telling them to her sister.

"Samantha," Sedgwick was hesitant and quiet with his next few words. "Her suicide was not your fault."

"I know that," Samantha was quick to respond. "It's just if I had of known. If she had told me what she was thinking, I could have stopped her." And in the café Samantha began to let the tears flow. Sedgwick got up from his chair and moved to her. He wrapped his arms around his friend to comfort her.

"There is no way you could have known. No one did. That is the secrecy of suicide. If they tell no one, no one can stop them."

"The rest of my family blames me. They think I should have known. As if being a twin meant that I had some sixth sense that I could have used to read her mind and stop her before she took her own life."

"I know Samantha. I am sorry. Everyone expresses grief in different ways. They are just trying to make sense of it all. Everyone is. Including you."

Samantha looked up at her friend. She hadn't remembered him being so wise. His words made sense. They didn't want to make her return home. For she knew she was a long way from facing her family again. But she knew that one day they would have to talk all of this through. She sat upright. Somewhat relieved at lessening the burden of saying her sister's name once more.

"You don't have to have all the answers just yet Samantha," Sedgwick continued, "I just plead with you, to not rush into things with this stranger just because he fills the gap that Sarah and your father have left behind."

Samantha nodded. She knew her friend just wanted the best for her and some of what he was proposing made complete sense to her. She had avoided feeling the pain that she knew was just bottled up in her heart. She also knew that when she was around David, the pain felt less intense. The ache was always there, but the loneliness dissipated. She wondered if Sedgwick might be correct about filling a void.

"I need sleep," she finally responded. She had much to think about but needed a fully functioning brain to do so.

"Get some sleep," Sedgwick agreed. "Tonight, we have dinner and drinks with some clients." Sedgwick suddenly smiled as a memory came back to him. "And if you want to make some travel money, one of our friends from last night requested your company."

Samantha was shocked at the suggestion. "No thank you Sedgwick! No judgment or anything, but I am definitely not your girl for the job."

* * *

The dinner conversation later that night turned once more to the concept of soulmates as Samantha proposed her forming beliefs to the group of businessmen.

"This theory of yours is ridiculous, Samantha. This idea that you have just one romantic soulmate. This one person who you are destined to be with." Sedgwick debated passionately as he attempted to debunk Samantha's romantic notion of a soulmate. "Just think about it, what if your soulmate lived across the world and the two of you never met. The chances of not meeting your one true love are far greater than the chance of ever meeting them."

Samantha nodded. She couldn't disagree with that fact.

"But what if the universe ensured that the two of you met, like David and I? The universe put us together once before we realised what it was trying to tell us."

"Then that my dear, that is a far more dangerous theory than even the concept of soulmates. What you are suggesting now is a pre-determined destiny already fated, by a mystical all-knowing being. Is that really how you want to imagine your life to be? A pre-programmed schedule of events and people that you have no choice over."

Samantha thought about her response. "But we still have choice don't we. David and I both chose not to say anything to each other in the Temple in Vietnam. We both could have spoken and didn't."

"But then this universe of yours, so determined to fate the two of you together, placed you both in Rome at the very same time to meet again. Where is the choice in that?"

The American businessman from the group spoke next, "Well I think we all make our own destiny. We create what we want in our lives through intention and hard work."

Samantha addressed her new acquaintance, "Have you heard the saying that everything happens for a reason? Haven't you ever felt like some things play out exactly as they need to without any input from yourself?"

He responded without a moment's hesitation, "If you believe that you wouldn't be here."

"Why do you say that?" Samantha was curious to find out what this businessman with the thick accent and commanding presence meant by his statement. She paused and waited for his thoughts to fall from his mouth.

"Well if you truly believed everything happens for a reason, you would be with your soulmate right now instead of here with us."

Samantha bowed her head in sadness at the mention of her David and the reason behind his absence right now. She wasn't sure how much was appropriate to share with her dinner companions for the evening.

"It is complicated for us right now."

Sedgwick took the opportunity to fill in the missing information for his friends. "David, her soulmate has had some loss in his life recently."

"Oh, I am sorry to hear that," the polite American replied.

Sedgwick continued, "He lost both parents quite suddenly and unexpectedly."

The American considered the information carefully before turning again to Samantha. "And how do you explain that with your theory that everything happens for a reason?"

She simply shook her head. There was no explaining the terrible tragedy of David's parents' deaths except for a cruel twist of fate by an evil and heartless universe.

"I can't," she finally admitted, both to the curious companions and to herself. There was no rational explanation for the loss of two much loved parents in such a short space of time.

"Maybe there is a large inheritance," one of the quieter members of the group finally suggested.

"Or possibly he will propose marriage to you, so heartbroken by his loss. The need for something, anything to fill the void," a man of European descent suggested the not-so-romantic offer of marriage as an explanation.

Sedgwick laughed at the suggestion. "And Samantha would reject such a ridiculous offer. Wouldn't you Samantha?"

Sedgwick looked to his friend now for confirmation that she understood how truly ridiculous a notion of marriage would be right now to her supposed soulmate.

Samantha couldn't respond for in her most private of thoughts, she had dreamt of marrying David. She had laid in bed missing his warmth and wondered what it would be like to spend every night together. She had wondered if he had thoughts about it too. The long stretches of time not hearing from David had her question the very nature of soulmates, but now with his arrival imminent she was able to once more imagine what their future held. She allowed her daydreams to conjure up images of a small family, two children, a boy and a girl. Her handsome husband lifting them up one in each arm to smother them with kisses. She dared not tell anyone of her fantasy life. She responded to the table with silence.

Sedgwick turned his attention to his friend once more. "Samantha, please tell me you are not thinking of doing anything as stupid as marrying this man."

Samantha felt an overwhelming sadness engulf her. "Please, can we not do this now?" She swallowed back the coming tears. "Let's drink. I need another beer," she shouted to the table. A resounding clunk of glasses as the group agreed wholeheartedly to the idea of getting the celebrations back on track with more alcohol.

Fourteen

Berlin, Germany

The snow was falling continually in Berlin. With it bringing a magical feel of a fresh start. The icy streets played havoc with the late-night revellers who left the dinner to explore the bar scene in the busy city streets of this German city. Samantha stopped and looked skyward. The sting of the cold crystals as they landed on her exposed skin a pleasant contrast to the warm heating inside the various venues they had visited that night. She stuck out her tongue and let the delicate ice particles stick to her mouth.

Sedgwick came to stand beside Samantha, arms outstretched. He followed her lead and let his tongue catch the falling snow. Samantha turned to face him.

"Isn't it just magical!" she enthused.

"Just magical," Sedgwick replied, the mocking tone fun-loving and harmless. "Are you sure you don't want to make some money tonight?" Sedgwick proposed the deal to her again.

Samantha looked at him, not certain at first as to what he was referring to, until a moment later the recognition hit her.

"No!" She raised her voice so the message was clear and expressed without a hint of doubt. "Absolutely not! There is no way I could do that!"

"The American has asked several times already. He is quite taken by you," Sedgwick informed her.

"Sedgwick, I don't know how you do it."

"It's quite easy Samantha really. Give it a go."

"But what about love. Don't you want to meet someone and fall in love one day?"

"I fall in love every other day, my sweet naïve friend. I fell in love with the apple strudel we just had for dessert in fact." He smiled as he recalled the delicious soft pastry and the spicy apple filling of the divine ending to his meal.

"I'm serious. Don't you want to meet your soulmate?" Samantha was certain she could convince her friend of her theory with enough encouragement.

"I have!"

His response shocked Samantha to learn.

"Who?"

"You!" he paused, "The American, the gorgeous Italian man I have booked again for next week in Rome, the Australian entrepreneur who is flying me first class to Dubai for his business trip."

"They aren't soulmates Sedgwick. They are clients." Samantha opposed his carefree use of the word.

"Who is to say who is and isn't my soulmate. I don't believe the same as you Samantha. I don't prescribe to this notion of one romantic soulmate. I have many. I fall in love over and over again. We are all capable of loving more than one person. That is why we can have more than one soulmate." He paused to consider before continuing, "I have soulmates scattered around the globe and so do you!"

Samantha shook her head. She didn't want to believe it to be true. "No, it isn't like that for me. I haven't felt this way before. What I feel for David. It is unique. It can't be replicated."

Sedgwick was thoughtful once more. On one hand, he was happy that Samantha had finally found love but on the other hand, he couldn't help but question the timing of this unlikely love match.

"Samantha, maybe your heart finally opened to the possibility of love. That is why David is the first to have touched you in such a way. But maybe he is just the start of many, many romances yet to come."

Samantha did not want to believe it. She hoped that David was truly the one but she knew in all reality that only time would tell. Time was after all, the ultimate decider.

* * *

David's arrival in Berlin was a mere few hours after Samantha farewelled her old friend, Sedgwick for his journey to Rome. She was thankful that her two men didn't meet. Sedgwick's unease about her soulmate theory had made her feel uncomfortable. She knew it didn't apply for her but she couldn't help but realise that love and soulmates meant something different to each person, which meant that even her and David could have different understandings of the same concept. His final words to her rang through her ears. He begged her to think about what they had discussed. He urged her to consider talking to someone about the loss of her much-loved sister. He tried to make her promise to take her time and work her way through the grieving process before getting into anything too serious with David.

Samantha appreciated his words but was grateful to now have this time together with David to finally explore what might lie ahead for the two of them. She understood her friend's concern but wanted to focus on the positives in her life and a future that until a short time ago she had never imagined possible.

Samantha waited in her spacious Berlin apartment, David having made her promise to not venture out in the heavy snow just to meet him. The door buzzer sounded and she ran the few steps to it.

"Hello?" her voice rang through the microphone to her waiting lover below.

"Guten Morgen," David sang back through the system. Samantha's smile grew as she realised her lover was now just metres away.

"Third floor," she instructed him. She ran to the bathroom for one final check in the mirror. She was glowing. Sedgwick was right. She had lost some weight since David had seen her last and the annoying cough she had carried since Rome had persisted. But today her face was alight, she couldn't wipe the smile from her face and she was beyond excited to see her soulmate once more.

She opened the door just as David raised his hand to knock. She threw her arms around him. That familiar heat rose immediately in her body as her lover dropped his bag to wrap her in his arms. Lifting her feet off the ground, he picked her up and brought her mouth to his. Their kiss was yearning. So long had the lovers waited for this moment, that they did not want to tear apart. David squeezed his lover, his strong arms contracting to hold her tight. He noticed her fragility and loosened his grip.

Samantha, hungry for the touch of his skin found the end to his shirt and placed her hands on the bare skin of his back. She instantly felt the excitement rise inside her as she remembered what it was like to touch her lover. She was eager to bring him inside the warmth of her apartment to continue the foreplay. She released her mouth from his and took his hand to direct him inside. He stopped her, bringing her back to the doorway. He paused for a moment longer and stared at her beautiful hazel eyes, her long dark hair and her soulful smile.

"Marry me!" he blurted out. "I love you. I don't ever want to be apart again." He barely took a breath before he repeated the fateful words again, "Marry me!"

Samantha shook her head in disbelief. She wasn't sure what she was hearing from the lips of her lover. She looked at his eyes, pleading for a response from her. Her mind wanted to do a thousand calculations. So many combinations of words raced through her brain. For a moment, she didn't know which ones to choose.

"Yes!" her heart chose for her. She felt at the same time fearful and relieved at her acceptance of the impromptu proposal.

"Yes?" David looked at her, his back hunched down to stare straight into the eyes of his lover. "Did you say yes?" It was as if he couldn't believe the words that fell from her mouth.

"Yes, I will marry you David," she reassured that he understood correctly.

He grabbed her once more in his arms, lifting her from the ground, he swung her body around and around. "Yes!" he sang out into the empty corridor. "Yes!" he repeated again.

She landed on the floor with a sudden jolt. Her mind raced with thoughts and her body shook with excitement. She grabbed David by the hand once more. "Let's go and make babies," she smiled sexily at him.

"I thought you would never ask," David replied. He reached down and grabbed his bag before following Samantha inside. When the front door of the apartment was closed, the bag once more fell to the floor. Samantha with all of her strength pressed David against the door and wasted no time in finding the front of his shirt. She ran her fingers inside the warm material to feel his hard abdominal muscles against the soft palms of her hands. Her willing companion grabbed at her own shirt, pulling it in one movement over her head. He felt for his scarf and threw it on the ground. He removed his beanie from his head and tossed it into the large room.

Samantha moved her hands onto his jacket and pushed it over his shoulders, forcing it to fall from his arms and onto the ground beneath him. Unbuttoning his shirt with expert precision, she couldn't wait to feel his warm skin against hers. She stood in awe at the beautiful specimen in front of her. She had missed his hard torso against her. She urgently needed to be close to him. She found the tag of the zipper of his jeans and began to undo the fastening.

He reached down and grabbed the cheeks of her petite bottom with both hands and drew her body up onto his waist. She wrapped her legs and arms around him as he took his first steps down the corridor of the apartment. Her mouth was hard against his. She lifted one hand and pointed toward the doorway that led to the queen-sized bed.

He stepped inside the room and without pausing gently placed his beloved Samantha on the bed. He lay on top of her, pushing his body hard against hers. He had thought of this moment the entire flight to reach her. Unable to stop himself, he peeled her jeans from her legs and removed the final piece of fabric to reveal his naked lover. He needed to feel her once more. He removed his jeans quickly. He crawled onto the bed. Paused above his now fiancé, he kissed her lips once more.

"I love you more than you could ever imagine."

Fifteen

Berlin, Germany

The lovers woke in each other's arms, content and exhausted from their lustful reunion. Samantha kissed David's chest and the soft, dark hair tickled her now sensitive lips. He leant his head down and kissed her forehead.

"David?" Samantha pondered her next question. "How many children do you want?"

He smiled at the question. He could hardly believe his dreams were coming true.

"Besides the one we just made?" He chuffed at the thought of it.

"Besides the one we possibly maybe just created," Samantha agreed with him. "How many more?"

David didn't have an answer for the question. He hadn't imagined his future family finally being within reach. For one heartbreaking moment, he remembered his parents and imagined the incredible grandparents they would have made, given the chance. He wanted to honour them.

"Let's not stop. Let's have as many children as we can," he replied excitedly.

"You will be an amazing father," Samantha promised him. She knew now that there was no doubt in her mind. She knew that this was her future. She would not doubt it a second longer.

"And you will be an incredible mother," David responded.

He knew in his heart that this caring, beautiful woman in his arms would be the soulmate that he would grow old with. The love of his life who would with him raise a home full of children, watch on as they grow and begin their own families. He couldn't wait for their lives to begin.

"Sam, let's go and feed you. I don't think you have been eating well since I left you. And our baby is going to need his mother to be healthy and strong."

"His mother?" Samantha questioned him, "Are you already planning on a son?" she teased him.

"Boy or girl. I don't mind at all. But a son to protect his younger sisters would be a good idea. So, let's go eat." David began to make the motion of rising from the bed.

"I'm not hungry my love." Samantha paused before adding her flirty suggestion, "Not for food anyway."

David instantly felt his hardness. His lover had an incredible effect on him.

"What are you hungry for, my love?"

Samantha raised her head to look at his eyes. "Just you."

David kissed her soft lips. She licked the edge of his mouth ensuring he completely understood her intent behind her sexy words.

"Let's be certain you completed the necessary task at hand, shall we? Let's try to make that son of yours. One more time?"

* * *

Having indulged in an entire afternoon in the apartment, eating, making love and catching up, Samantha and David were keen for an early start the following day to make their way to the East Side Gallery. The remnants of the Berlin Wall had long been on the list of landmarks Samantha had wanted to see in the world and she was not disappointed. The lovers spent hours walking the icy paths on either side of the wall, stopping often to take photos of brightly coloured pieces of street art that adorned the concrete barrier.

"Look at that," Samantha pointed to the bright blue turquoise patch of the wall, the handwritten quote unreferenced but meaningful: 'Lose every sense of time.' Samantha read the words out loud to her lover. "That idea, that concept about time keeps coming up again and again."

"That's because it is true." David understood more than anyone the importance of the time and making every minute count."

"What does it mean to you?" Samantha was keen to learn more about her lover's philosophical thoughts of the world. She knew he was an incredibly spiritual and thoughtful person and she wanted to begin to learn every last thing about him.

David was still for a moment, thinking of exactly the thoughts and feelings behind what the words meant to him. He could sense this was something on Samantha's mind at the moment, so he wanted to ensure he treated the topic with the respect it deserved.

"I think it means stop waiting for the right time. Embrace this very second in time and do what makes you happy" David paused. "Or something along those lines."

Samantha took in the words and stared at the wall. She wasn't sure if this was what the original author meant. She had no idea if this quote was a well-known one or a pondering scribbled by a local student. For some reason, there was a message in the messy black letters that she needed to hear.

"Maybe it means we should forget the concept of counting time altogether. It is after all a man-made construct, this idea of time. Measured by instruments designed to dictate our day down to the smallest of increments. Maybe we are to abandon time as we know it."

They took a step back from the wall as if the words themselves grew in size, no longer able to be contained within the cement encasing them.

David took his lover's hand and kissed the back of her palm. He truly loved this side to Samantha; the thoughtful artist who challenged every concept to find true meaning and purpose in her world. This is the Samantha that he long ago had fallen in love with; even if he wasn't sure back that this thing was called love. He knew his Samantha had made a mark on his soul that would stay with him forever. David too stared at the wall. He pondered a world without time.

"What difference would it make if we failed to mark the day with a twenty-four-hour passing? What chaos would consume the world? The sun would still set at night and rise in the morning. The tides would still know when to encroach the shore and when to recede. The earth would still turn as it circles around the sun. We would rise with the daybreak without even caring what the clock beside our bed deemed it to be," Samantha pondered.

David liked Samantha's view of the passing of time and had an exciting idea. "What about if we mark our life with moments instead of time?"

Samantha smiled at her lover. She saw the sparkle in his eyes as the idea began to take hold.

"I love it! So instead of the year 2016 when we were in Berlin together, this point in our lives now becomes the moment you knocked me up." Samantha laughed at the idea. It was frivolous and carefree just like their relationship.

"Moments and places," David added. We mark our life by the moments that were special and the places that were special to us. We have a huge map on the wall of our dining room. Every time we eat a meal we sit and remember the moments and places we have visited. We bore our children and grandchildren with stories of our great love affair."

"I love you David for even thinking of that!" Samantha had another idea. "We put pins in the map for the places we have been together. Let's aim to mark off the world by the time we grow old."

David laughed and threw his head back. "We have green pins for the places we have visited and red pins for the places we made love."

Samantha roared with laughter. "This poor map will be covered by the time we are finished. We have already covered Rome, Florence and Berlin. We have to go back to Hanoi, where we saw each other and collect a red pin there."

The lifelong plan for the couple came together effortlessly. Sharing their lives, exploring the world together.

"What about if we make love on a plane over an ocean?"

"We mark the location to the best of our ability," David explained.

"Our poor children." Samantha wasn't entirely sure their future children needed to know that much information about their parents.

They moved along the wall and to an art piece in French. Samantha could make out a few words but the linguist of the pair translated much more.

"This is about war," David began to explain. "It is about a soldier who is injured and dying. He is lying down amongst the dead bodies and waiting for his death. But suddenly, when the night is starting to fall, he begins to smile as he imagines escaping from this hell."

He turned to his lover to see tears in her eyes. He wrapped his arms around her and kissed her forehead. There was no need for words of comfort. He knew Samantha well enough to know that she wanted to feel the emotions as they came to her. She no longer wanted to run from anything that hurt her

Once more holding Samantha in his arms, he was reminded of her fragility. Stress can be a debilitating trigger for ill health. He felt pure anguish for the agony he put Samantha through with his long absence and days of little or no communication. He owed it to her to make it up to her. To now care for her every day for the rest of their lives. He wanted to make her feel safe and loved and never again fearful or stressed.

David looked to the woman he loved. He had a new idea forming in his mind. "Let's return to Rome. Let's get married where we once more met."

"I do!" Samantha whispered to her lover. "I mean, yes, I will, in Rome." She stood on her toes and reached up to kiss her future husband on the lips. "I can't wait to be your wife."

They stood in silence staring at the impressive wall in front of them. The hundreds of philosophical images and words each more meaningful than the last.

"There is something else I really want to see first though before we return to Rome," Samantha spoke through the silence, still not breaking the hold between them.

"Anything my darling," David was quick to comply to her request. He didn't even need to know more. He would follow his love anywhere in the world that she wanted to go.

"Do you fancy a quick trip to Spain?" Samantha looked up at her lover.

"Of course," David agreed wholeheartedly.

Sixteen

Barcelona, Spain

The sound of the seatbelt lights being turned off rang and David turned to Samantha.

"Want to go now?" His wicked grin spread from ear to ear.

"Go where?" Samantha wasn't entirely sure she grasped the meaning of the invitation.

"Mile high club?" he whispered in her ear so the fellow passenger occupying the window seat of their row didn't hear them.

"You're not serious, are you?" Samantha asked as she let out a nervous giggle.

"Moments!" David smiled back at her. "It's all about the moments we create, remember?"

Samantha didn't need any further encouragement. She was going to finally live her life one moment to the next. She took her lover's hand and stepped over his legs to make her way to the aisle. She gave him a cheeky grin and pulled him from his seat. There was no doubt to anyone in that plane of what Samantha was taking her lover to do. She walked proudly down the centre row of the plane, her hand grasping his. She walked straight to the lavatory cubicle, pushed it open, thrust David inside and locked the door.

The giggling from behind the locked bathroom door was unashamed. Envious couples that overheard glanced at each other. None, game enough to take the plunge into the mile-high club for themselves.

The couple made it back to their seats in time for the meal service. A croissant filled with ham and cheese, a juice and a white wine for each of them. David pondered his lover's choice of beverage. "What if you are pregnant already? Maybe you shouldn't be drinking."

For a moment Samantha's breath caught in her throat. As much as she loved the idea of falling pregnant immediately, she hadn't given much thought to the practicalities of what she should do when it actually happened. Samantha would be the first of her family to fall pregnant. The eldest of three girls now. Her sister's death leaving her the prominent place as the eldest child on her own for the first time in her life. Moments like now made her feel so very alone without her beloved twin.

Although not a parent herself, Sarah would have known what to do. She would have made it up even if she didn't. She would have googled the information, she would have dragged Samantha to the book store and piled her arms full of parenting books. She would have taken her home and together the two of them would have read and re-read every important page until together they had all the answers they needed.

Samantha put her hand to her stomach. The deep sense of loss made her stomach muscles tighten and contract. It might have been the flight or it might have been the airline food but something had suddenly made Samantha feel a little off-colour. She looked toward David. "Can I put my head on your shoulder please?" she asked her lover.

He lifted his hand to the side of her head and lowered it to place it gently on his shoulder. He turned his mouth to kiss her forehead. "You feel a little warm. Are you ok?" he asked, his concern for his lover difficult to mask.

She watched as his arm went up to find the vent above them. He turned the circular dial to the right to allow the free flow of air to fall on her face below. Neither Samantha nor David had any way of knowing that this exact moment, was the moment that they would cherish forever, the creation of their first child

By the time the plane landed in Barcelona, Samantha had made nearly a full recovery. She was ready for more adventures with the man she loved. Their first stop was the tiny hotel on Ronda de Sant Pere where they were scheduled to spend just a few short nights before flying back to Rome for their impending marriage.

The hotel was not as expected. The supposed spa pool drained of any water due to a technical malfunction. The outdoor sun deck, a bare timber flooring housing two rickety pieces of plastic outdoor furniture. The lobby had a strange odour to it. Not quite distinguishable but highly detectable to the human sense of smell. David was keen to find somewhere more suitable for his bride-to-be but Samantha wanted to drop her bags and begin exploring the vibrant tourist district of this impressive city.

They ventured down the road toward the harbour when Samantha smelt the most delicious scent. A freshly baked paella was being served to the alfresco table adjoining the nearby café. The mouthwatering meal was fragrant and bursting with fresh vegetables drowning in a bed of golden liquid rice. She stopped in her tracks and looked to her lover. "You hungry?" she enquired.

"Yes, and I am so glad to see you finally are." The couple took the nearest table and begun studying the menu. The waiter appeared to welcome the tourists to his little piece of the world.

"Sangria to start with?" The waiter tempted them with the beverage of choice in Spain.

David looked to Samantha for confirmation.

"I just might have a sparkling water," Samantha suggested. "But you go ahead and have one and tell me how delicious it is." David looked to the waiter to confirm the order of just one sangria.

Once the waiter left, David turned his concentration to Samantha once more. "Do you think you might be…?" His voice trailed off.

Samantha smiled. She understood exactly what David was hoping for.

"Of course, I couldn't know yet. It's a bit early to tell if I am actually pregnant. But we can definitely keep trying." She giggled a little at the thought of making love to her gorgeous David. Penises and time, these two thoughts kept reoccurring in her conversations. She made a mental note to write a blog about it as soon as she found a spare hour.

The huge meals arrived and the paella tasted as amazing as it looked. David finished his meal in a short space of time and watched Samantha struggle to even consume half of hers.

"Feeling unwell again?" His assessment of her change in appetite raised concern once more for him about the woman he loved.

"Just not as hungry as I thought I was," Samantha admitted, grabbing at her stomach once more to indicate her fullness.

"Once we get you back to Rome, I am booking you in with a doctor. I have a friend who will see you as soon as we land." David's tone was firm and he made it obvious he wasn't looking for confirmation.

Samantha was thankful she had a man in her life that cared for her in the way David did. This was new to her and she was aware it would take some time to get used it to but she was encouraged that this love was something she could grow into.

* * *

The next morning, the couple woke once more in each other's arms. Samantha had never slept better than since she had known David. She bounced out of bed ready to visit the magnificent Basilica de la Sagrada Familia. Long had she yearned to venture into the remarkable old building. Over a hundred and thirty years old and still many years from completion. The line outside was long and slow as the hordes of tourists crisscrossed the concrete allotment beside the ticket booth to purchase their pass for the day. Samantha didn't waste a moment in the line as she peered at every conceivable ornate detail of the incredible building. The facade from where they waited so detailed in its design, not an inch of it appeared untouched by the great architect.

The story of Antoni Gaudi, the passionate architect behind the church was a fascinating one. Wanting to build a church large enough to house the city's entire family, he set out to create a masterpiece. His talent revered by many, his devotion to his work inspiration for the flood of donations that would follow, decades even, after his death in 1926. His untimely demise a sad event for the city. Crossing the street outside the church he was struck by a streetcar. Dressed so modestly he was mistaken for a homeless beggar and taken to the morgue unidentified for the immediate future. A man who was not impressed by wealth but rather by the value of a person. He was a great man who created an incredible gift for future generations.

The church now stood as a testament to his vision of creating a place to welcome all. The religion it stands to preach without denomination. Finally, as the couple took their entry tickets in their hand, they made their way up the few stairs to take in the beauty close up. Samantha clicked away, the camera barely leaving her face as she found one indescribable piece of design after the other.

Her fingertips traced the hard surface of the exterior of the building. Her touch, a valuable sense in connecting with the history of the warm materials. She took David's hand to step through the massive archway of the front door. They stopped frozen with the awe-struck beauty of the sight before them. Simultaneously they let out a sound of amazement. Samantha giggled at the pair of them.

"This is…" she tried to find the words.

"I know…" David himself, the man of many words was baffled into silence.

"I have never seen anything like it," Samantha confessed.

"Me neither," David agreed.

"This is a moment!" Samantha took the time to mark yet another special point in time for the lovers.

He grabbed her in his arms. "I love you more than you could ever imagine," he promised his lover. He needed to mark this moment with the declaration of his undying love for this woman. "Thank you for bringing me here."

"My pleasure," Samantha assured him.

The couple stayed joined together for a long time, content in standing still and taking in the atmosphere of the inspiring interior of the old church, and they were not alone. Every person who stepped through the doorway gasped in disbelief at the sight that welcomed them. Young children, old men, each and every one did not fail to express their genuine amazement at the beauty and serenity held within the walls of the impressive building.

Samantha and David stepped through the quiet interior to gaze at the beauty of the stain-glassed windows. The colours of the rainbow vibrant in each and every pane. The sun blazed through the translucent glass casting over the interior sprays of colours, each more spectacular than the last. The synchronicity of the window panes, the complexity of the patterns, random but at the same time formed to complement each other, held the couples' stare for what seemed like an eternity.

Samantha led her willing companion to the centre of the church. There they found a seat on the hard wooden pews in front of the altar. Samantha looked skyward to the most impressive ceiling she had ever seen. She tapped David on the arm indicating for him to take in the sight. She let her head fall over the back of the seat to take in the scene. David followed, taking her hands in his as he did so.

"This is just amazing. Look at that detail," she said to him.

"This has to be one of the most beautiful things I have ever seen," he agreed with her.

"Are we having another moment?" Samantha teased her good-looking companion.

"I think we are," David whispered back to her. The quiet in the great church filled by so many excited tourists was testament to the respect they held for both the venue and the great man whose vision it was to create this space of worship for the masses.

"Do you know what I think this moment is about?" David teased Samantha, waiting to see if she would take the bait and hear his words of ponderings.

"Of course," Samantha reassured him.

She loved hearing David's philosophical ideals. The moment took her back to the catacombs of Rome and her memory of watching David as he guided the tourists through the historical ruins of the ancient city. She remembered listening in awe as David shared his well thought out and highly held beliefs about all religions basically being the same. She wondered what David might have to add now about his thoughts on what this moment in time stood for.

"This moment is about showing us the importance of leaving a legacy." He let the words sink in. "This church, this place of worship for everyone, lives long after the man who created it. Gaudi created something that would live on forever."

Samantha knew exactly what David was referring to. "You are talking about children, aren't you?"

David smiled at her, "You know it."

She smiled back. Everything lately came back to their desire to start a family. She took David in her arms. "You are giving it one hundred percent effort. You know. This making a baby idea," she giggled.

"You know me!" he laughed at himself.

Seventeen

Rome, Italy

The return to Rome came around much quicker than the couple had anticipated. And with the return came two events that had Samantha both excited and nervous with anticipation. David, as promised had booked her an appointment with a doctor that he trusted and respected. A female doctor in the hope that Samantha would feel comfortable both now and into the future as a potential pregnancy progressed.

Samantha loved David's little home in Rome. It was everything she imagined it to be. Both masculine and full of character yet welcoming, comforting even. The whole place had the very scent of him entrenched in its being. She fell into his soft bed, pleased to think that she had a place to call home now after so many weeks of living out of a suitcase, moving from one temporary residence to the next.

David lay beside her, turned onto his side and propped himself up by his arm as he did. He placed his spare hand on Samantha's stomach.

"Do you want me to come to the doctor with you?" He wanted Samantha to feel in full control over her medical visit but he secretly wished for her to invite him along for the appointment.

"No, I would rather go on my own. You know, it's just one of those things." She disappointed him with her answer.

"I understand. I just know how you feel about medical venues and hospitals."

Samantha cringed at the memories those words conjured up. She had spent enough time in hospitals and around doctors for the time being. She had only really agreed to the check-up to placate David. She knew he had been worried about her and she wanted to put his mind at ease.

"You do know I have been feeling so much better with you around. My cough has improved and I swear I have gained some of the weight that I had lost."

"I am sure you will here in Rome. Every night pasta and pizza, the best in the world. Not to mention your favourite, the gelato."

"Mmm, gelato, let's go and get some now."

David looked at his lover and licked his lips, you know what I would prefer to gelato right now?"

And a second later, Samantha hungered for exactly the same thing. The couple made love slowly, taking the time to explore each other's bodies. Finding new ways to pleasure each other, over and over again.

* * *

Samantha slept in the following day and woke to find David already gone. She searched her brain for a memory recalling where he said he might have taken off to so early. She reached over for her phone just as the bedroom door opened.

David emerged, a huge smile on his face, his arms full of white paper bags filled with delicious smelling goodies.

"Breakfast for my wife-to-be!" He waved the bags around slightly to let the aroma of the breakfast calzone seep into her senses.

She immediately sat up in bed, hungry for the delightful banquet she was about to enjoy.

"And do I smell coffee?" she asked hopefully.

He sat down beside her and began to lay the food out carefully on a tray he collected from beneath the mattress.

"Coffee first, I will assume?"

"Of course, my dear. Always coffee first," she agreed with him. "And what else do we have? It looks like you have bought out the entire café."

"I need to look after my future wife now, don't I?" he explained his extravagance away.

He had finished laying out the breakfast in front of her when she noticed one small parcel left.

"What's in that one?" she was curious to know the contents of the mystery bag.

"That one my dear is freshly made gelato, hazelnut and coffee. I think you should start with this one first before it melts."

Samantha couldn't resist the temptation of gelato at any time of the day. David handed her the parcel and the spoon and found his own coffee to take a small sip. Samantha opened the bag and the divine combination of creamy coffee and smooth hazelnut danced with her tastebuds. She took her first mouthful and closed her eyes as she licked the spoon clean for every last morsel.

David watched on with pleasure as Samantha enjoyed her creamy breakfast dessert. He watched as her expression changed. He followed her eyes to see the shiny emerald ring emerge from the frothy substance. She lifted her spoon to her eyes as David watched on in silence. A grin formed on his face and he was pleased he was able to surprise his Samantha.

Still holding the spoon full of gelato and jewellery in the air, Samantha turned her head to face David.

"What?"

David reached over and took the ring from the gelato. He placed it directly in his mouth and gently sucked the sweet substance clean from the white gold that encased the precious gem. As he raised his hand to his mouth, the now clean ring emerged, more glistening and magnificent than before.

He held the ring out for Samantha to see it. She looked at the gift and then back to David.

"Samantha Cleary. Will you marry me?"

Samantha placed her spare hand over her mouth. "David!" she gushed. "You didn't have to."

David smiled at her. "Now, is when you say, yes, normally that is how this works."

"Yes, yes, yes!" Samantha yelled as she leapt up from her seated position to kneel on the bed beside her lover to kiss him deeply on his lips. She pulled her head away and noticed the ring still in David's hand, still outstretched waiting for its final resting place. Samantha gave her hand to David and he slowly ran the ring the length of her finger, never for a moment taking his eyes off his most beloved Samantha.

He leant forward and kissed her on the mouth once more. Using the distraction to reach for the gelato bowl squeezed in Samantha's right hand. "And I will have some of this now too if you don't mind sharing." He laughed a little at how happy he was.

Samantha relinquished the gelato to sit down again and examine the sensational ring that adorned her left hand. She looked up once more and noticed that the gelato was being demolished at a rate of seconds. He noticed her eyes as they glanced at the delicious treat. He teasingly dipped the spoon into the substance, taking with it the largest spoonful he could manage. He lifted the spoon to his mouth as his watched Samantha's mouth drop. He laughed again at the naïve innocence of his lover. He took the spoon and placed it gently in her mouth. She closed her lips and let the divine taste once again slide down her throat.

* * *

The time had come to leave the warm confines of her new little home to make her way across the city for the visit to her doctor. She had brief ideas about not going at all. Of telling David she was feeling much better and that she had decided to wait a while before seeking any professional medical advice. But for David and for the child she would hope to one day carry, she would make the visit for a check-up and listen to whatever advice or recommendations the doctor might have for her.

She entered the waiting room of the doctor's office to find it empty. For a moment, she considered that it might actually be closed. The reception desk was abandoned and there were no sounds from behind the wall that led to the doctor's private appointment room. She took the few steps inside the door and a friendly face emerged.

"Bonjourno," the smiling medical receptionist welcomed her.

"Um, hello," Samantha replied, "Um, I only speak English, is that ok?" she added.

"Yes, yes of course. You must be Samantha," the confident woman concluded.

"Yes, I have an appointment."

"Yes, of course, come straight through. The doctor is looking forward to seeing you." Samantha couldn't believe how incredibly friendly the welcome was and the lack of waiting or crowded reception areas was a welcome change to the bulk billing medical services of home.

Samantha followed the kind receptionist through the door and into a small corridor that housed, from what she could tell just another three rooms or so. She hadn't thought to question how much this visit would cost and she started to imagine a service of this kind would not come cheaply.

The receptionist gave a slight tap on the door before turning the handle and motioning for Samantha to enter. Immediately the elderly doctor stood up from her seat and walked to Samantha. Samantha placed her hand out in greeting and was a little surprised when the doctor walked straight up to her and placed her arms around her, kissing first one cheek and then the next.

"Samantha, what a pleasure to meet you," the doctor announced as she pulled away. "I have heard only lovely things about you. Our David is quite taken by you I might say." The heavy Italian accent did not cover the genuine excitement this professional alluded to on greeting her new patient.

"Thank you, Doctor."

"Sofia, please call me Sofia," she insisted. "Now come along and take a seat and let's talk for a bit."

The following hour flew by with Samantha sharing more than she even intended to about not only her recent health concerns but the suicide death of her twin sister and the very serious talks about pregnancy that no one outside of her and David knew about.

At the end of the consult, Samantha had been given instructions to return on the same day the following week. Blood tests as well as full vitals had been taken and the results would be discussed at the next visit. As well as any preliminary precautions for pregnancy such as additional vitamins and a more regular diet plan for Samantha's weight gain.

All in all, it wasn't an unpleasant visit. As Samantha left the hospitality of the office and the cold winter air of Rome hit her face, she felt a real sense of relief at finally sharing some of the incredible story that had become her reality in just a short space of a year. She was a little relieved to hear that most couples take a while to fall pregnant for the first time, especially as they both increase in age.

There was of course no reason Samantha and David should have any problems with conceiving, the doctor just wanted to reassure Samantha to not feel disappointed if it didn't happen immediately.

Walking home down the Piazza Colonna, Samantha enjoyed the sights and sounds of the busy Italian capital. Tourists bustled down the busy road, flitting from one ancient landmark to the next. Locals looked skyward before opening their umbrellas as the cold rain began to fall once more. The precipitation was gentle unlike the torrential downpours Samantha was used to back home in her Australian summer. Forgetting her umbrella as she often did, Samantha made her way across the street to Galleria Alberto Sordi. She stood under the safety of the arched entry watching the pace of the city increase as the rain began to fall harder.

She glanced at the peculiar business being undertaken at the side entrance of the building. A sign now covered by rain hawking the promotion of fortunes being told. Fifty Euros seemed a steep price to hear the ramblings of a psychic but Samantha was intrigued. She stared at the spare chair sitting opposite the fortune teller. His large black umbrella shielding both himself and his potential customer from the rain. She wondered why both psychics persisted in working in the downpour. A romantic notion began to form in Samantha's mind and she bounded over to the spare chair and took a seat.

"Bonjourno," the fortune teller began.

"Bonjourno," Samantha replied, "Do you speak English?"

"Yes of course." The kind face looked at Samantha as if he was already seeing into her future. "And what do you want to know?"

Samantha didn't hesitate. She finally, once and for all wanted her answer on soulmates. "Love, family, my future," she demanded to hear the details of all of them.

The kind man gently took Samantha's hand and turned her palm to face him. He looked intently at the lines and indentations that told him the story of Samantha's life. He let go of her hand and lifted his finger to trace the line that ran down the centre of Samantha's palm. With his other hand, he held the large umbrella over Samantha and himself to shelter them both from the weather.

"This line," he began sharing. "This is your lifeline. It tells me how you will live."

"And what does it say?" Samantha was eager to get some answers.

"It tells me you will have one great love."

"One?" Samantha questioned the fortune teller. She was delighted for the confirmation that David was indeed her one true soulmate.

"And no children," he added.

There was a long pause before Samantha was able to respond.

"What?"

She couldn't understand what she had just heard. She didn't want to believe that she would not bare children for her beloved David. She couldn't imagine them together for the rest of their lives without the love of children and grandchildren to fill their home.

The kind, elderly man looked into Samantha's surprised glare. "I am sorry. Are children something you were hoping for?"

"Yes," Samantha said quietly.

He let out a long sigh. He realised his obvious mistake in saying too much too soon, but the reading from the palm was clear and most definite.

"I am sorry." He repeated the words, hoping they might ease the pain of the message just relayed.

"It's just that. We have been trying already for a baby. My fiancé and I. Samantha showed him the shiny emerald ring that adorned her wedding finger. She wanted the fortune teller to change his script. She silently begged for him to tell her he read it wrong. She looked into his eyes and pleaded for a different future than a future without children.

"I'm sorry. I truly am. I can only share with you what I can see."

Samantha slumped down in her chair, barely wanting to hear anything more from the man she huddled under the umbrella with. She glanced momentarily into the busy street. She wished for a moment, she could take back the last sixty seconds of her life. She turned to look once more at the man beside her.

"Do you wish to continue?" he asked of her.

"Yes," she responded without hesitation. The worst was surely past and she prayed for some more pleasant news from her future.

He took her hand once more and stared intently at the writings on her palm. "You will travel more," he informed her. "And soon. Somewhere warm. You love to travel."

Samantha couldn't argue with his latest assessment, but felt it was clearly a little vague considering her very strong Australian accent, which in the ancient city of Rome stood out amongst the crowds.

"You are creative, an artist maybe?"

"A blogger," Samantha informed him. "Not a very successful one. More of a hobby blogger really." She added the additional information for clarity.

"You will write more. One final piece. A great piece. It will bring you much fame."

"Really?" Samantha began to question the future that this man saw for her. "How is that so?" The information needed to make this infamy certain was at present beyond her grasp.

"I'm sorry. I do not know."

Samantha felt her unease rise. She wasn't exactly getting the information she had hoped that her fifty Euros would provide for her.
"Do you have any good news to share?"

He stopped and looked into her eyes once more. "I can only share what I see."

"And do you see anything positive. Some good news maybe?"

There was no delay in his response, "You are much loved."

Eighteen

Church of Santa Maria della Concezione dei Cappuccini, Rome.

Samantha considered the words she heard all the way home. She wasn't sure she should tell David for after all the musings of a street vendor were hardly proven scientific facts. She believed in her heart of hearts that her and David would become parents, and soon. She realised she had some part to play in it, getting herself healthy and well once more. Adhering to the meal plan that would help her gain the weight she had lost in David's absence was a start.

David had definitely been doing his best to support her increased eating. The gelato gifts hadn't stopped coming and the food in Italy was second to none. Some of Samantha's favourite, the Napoli pasta. A meal relying on the freshest of simple ingredients. The pizza, the scent of which drives people from the busy streets and into the sidewalk cafes to find it.

Life with David was pure joy from the moment she opened her eyes in the morning to the final kiss from her sweet love as she fell asleep, and she couldn't have been happier. Samantha let her mind often begin the planning of the wedding and each time she came back to the same idea. A simple wedding in Rome, just her and David, any witnesses they may need and a celebrant in an official capacity to legitimise it. In actual fact, the more Samantha thought about it, she didn't even require the marriage to be formal. It was not the legalities the lovers craved instead it was the opportunity to say the words of promise to one another.

With a further bit of research, Samantha came up with the perfect solution. She couldn't wait for David to return from his night-time tour of the catacombs to run the idea past him.

Already in bed and dozing after finishing another chapter of the latest book offering she had been given to review, Samantha's eyes opened the minute she heard David at the door.

"I'm home!" he yelled out into the dimly lit apartment. David had confessed this was his new favourite thing to do. Coming home each night to the woman he loved brought him immense pleasure. He was at times like a small child unable to hide his enthusiasm for life.

"I'm in bed and I have the best idea," Samantha yelled back to her fiancé.

"I like the sound of that!" David replied as he turned the corner to stand in the doorway to the bedroom. "What exactly, did you have in mind?" he teased her.

She smiled at his playfulness. How did life ever get to be this amazing. She paused for dramatic effect before beginning the presentation of her wedding planning.

"Marriage!" she beamed at her lover.

"Yes…" David walked the few steps to the bed to sit on the soft mattress beneath him.

"We can get married at the Church of Santa Maria della Concezione dei Cappuccini. The exact place you took me on the night we met again. I went by there today and asked if it was possible. They said they have a small chapel not open to the public but considering it was you, they were more than happy to let us use it."

Samantha paused and waited for David to reply.

"That explains a lot then." His suspicions were confirmed. "I wondered what was going on tonight. The staff at the church were all smiles and asking about you when I took the tour group through. I did think they were acting a little strange."

"They were so helpful and so very excited. I think they are planning on joining us for the ceremony." Samantha was happy to hear that no one gave the details away prior to her telling David herself. "There is one small hitch. I just don't know yet about the legalities of it all. It might be a wedding for ceremony's sake rather than a legal union. If that is ok with you? I mean we can always legalise it in the future, once we work out the details of how to do that given our current gypsy lifestyle that is."

David smiled a wide smile. "I love the idea and it is very thoughtful!" He leant forward and kissed her on the mouth. "And I have an idea too!" he flirted with her. The very tone in which he presented his thought, gave Samantha some idea as to what it might be. "How about we have our honeymoon in Iceland? In a glass roofed igloo under the Northern Lights. I know it is your dream to visit."

Samantha jumped up and straight on top of David. She pushed him down on the bed and kissed him repeatedly. "I love it. I love it!" she yelled out. Her excitement unable to be contained. She kissed him again and again.

David wrapped his strong arms around her and threw her onto the bed. Crawling on top of her, he stopped for a second to look into her eyes, "And I love you more than you could ever imagine," he hissed at her. They kissed more passionately than either of them ever thought possible. Something transcended between them. A certain knowing, a thought and emotion wrapped together into a mystical realisation that they had both finally found their one true romantic soulmate.

* * *

Samantha was the first to rise and quietly padded into the kitchen to brew her debut batch of Italian coffee for the day. She tried her best to be quiet so as not to wake the sleeping David. The coffee brewed and the addictive aroma filled their tiny home. Samantha closed her eyes and inhaled the warm scent of the coffee beans. Lost in the sensation she was pulled back to the present by the solid arms of her lover as they wrapped around her waist.

"Good morning my future wife," David purred at her from behind.

"Good morning my future husband," Samantha chimed back at him.

"I have an idea," David teased his lover.

"Mmm," Samantha didn't need to use her blogger's imagination to work out what it might be. "Let me guess," she began but was quickly interrupted.

"Let's get married today," David shocked her with his suggestion.

She quickly turned around to look at her lover's face, radiant with energy.

"Are you serious?"

"Yes, absolutely," he assured her. "I don't want to wait another day to call you my wife. It might not be legally binding, but that's not what this is about anyway. Let's have our beginning to the rest of our lives together."

Samantha didn't need any further convincing. She jumped up and wrapped her arms tightly around her lover's neck.

"Yes, yes. Let's do it."

Within hours, David and Samantha had secured the small chapel for the service, dressed and made their way to the venue. The elderly monk of the order had offered to say a few words of promise for them with the understanding that the service was a token gesture between the two rather than the binding agreement that they needed to complete one day in the not so distant future.

Samantha and David stood facing one another. Their hands clasped together as they spoke their promise to each other. Samantha was first and although she hadn't had the time to write what she wanted to say, the words came easily and with much emotion.

"David, on this day I take you to be my husband, my best friend, my lover and my soulmate. I could have never imagined the whirlwind that has been my life since I met you again right here in Rome. But at the same time, I feel as if we have always been together. I love you more than I ever thought I could love a man. You have made my life complete. I cannot wait to journey this life with you. You will be my last first kiss. That is my promise to you."

Samantha watched as David's eyes swelled with emotion. She spoke from her heart and although no words could truly describe the depth of her love for David, she had hoped that he heard in her promise the immense emotion she felt for him. It was David's turn.

"Samantha, today I take you to be my wife. The woman that I have loved since the day I first met you. We have journeyed through this life together but apart and never again will I leave your side. You are my one true love, my soulmate. I cannot wait to start our family together. I will grow old by your side. That is my promise to you. I love you more than you will ever know for no words can describe the love that I feel for you. You are my other half."

It was Samantha's turn to feel the words of her lover. She smiled at him. A small tear fell from her eye and ran down her cheek. David gently wiped it away with his finger.

The clergyman spoke, "And now for the purposes of this union, I ask David that you kiss your Samantha."

David leant forward and kissed Samantha delicately on the lips. A touch as light as a feather but with the intensity of an avalanche. "I love you," he whispered so the gathering and boisterous crowd of friends around them could not hear. These few words were just for her ears.

The friends gathered around with hugs and kisses to both cheeks to congratulate the couple. David's friends from his adopted home welcomed Samantha with open arms. So pleased were the Romans to witness such depths of love, they too wanted to be part of the great love story that unfolded before them.

"Limoncello!" one of David's friends yelled. The traditional drink of Rome was being poured immediately following the couple's promise to each other. The expatriates with their new friends took to the gesture with gusto. For this was a day of celebration. A day of new beginnings. A day that they would always remember.

Nineteen

Rome, Italy.

The wedding behind them, both were keen to start planning the honeymoon. An adventure in Iceland was something they had both yearned to explore for many years. Being able to do this together was something neither of them would have even imagined. A dream coming true. Daily life took over and David got back to his work as a tour guide while Samantha took to her blog and freelance work. Their life was simple, easy and better than either could have wished for.

The day came for Samantha to return to the doctor for her test results. She hadn't wanted to ring before the appointment. She was intent on waiting patiently to hear the outcome of her full blood work. She had been feeling more tired than ever and so far, hadn't managed to gain any of the weight she had lost even though she was feasting on the magnificent culinary delights that Italy offered in abundance.

She arrived at the quiet medical reception area and as her first visit was ushered into the doctor immediately. She walked into the neatly laid out office and was once more greeted with a friendly hug and kisses to both cheeks.

"Welcome," Doctor Sofia greeted her, "So lovely to see you again and I hear congratulations are in order as well."

"Yes, thank you." Samantha wondered how it was that the doctor knew of the nuptials, but was quickly realising Rome was in fact a very small place if you lived there. Everyone knew everyone and any news, good or bad travelled quickly.

"Take a seat Samantha please. I would like to talk to you," the doctor instructed her patient.

"Oh, that doesn't sound good." Samantha was instantly nervous at the news of the results. The doctor looked a little concerned and she wondered what she could possibly have to say to her. "What is it?"

"Well I have both good and bad news for you."

The statement hit Samantha hard.

"Go on please." It was better to hear it all straight away.

"Well, the good news is that you are indeed pregnant. Very early in your first trimester, but definitely you are now expecting."

Samantha wanted to cry. It was the best possible news she could receive. Especially given the fortune teller's foreboding prediction that she would never have children.

"Oh Sofia, that is wonderful news!" Samantha wanted to tell David straight away. She reached for her phone to ring her husband immediately with the good news.

The doctor reached over and with a gentle tap on Samantha's arm indicated for her to wait a moment before calling.

"Samantha, there is more news I need to share."

Samantha was instantly reminded of the second component of the test results. The so-called bad news.

"Go on." She sat silently waiting for the rest of the information to be relayed.

"Samantha, your blood tests indicated some abnormalities that require further investigation."

"Like what?" Samantha asked the doctor, concerned now more for her baby's health than her own. "Is it to do with the baby?" Samantha needed to know.

"No," the doctor assured her quickly.

"So, what is it?"

"I can't say for sure now, there are some abnormalities in your red blood count and it could be due to a number of reasons, we need further tests to find out for sure. I wouldn't want to alarm you by telling you much more at this stage."

"Alarm me?" The words fell from Samantha's mouth slowly as if the reality of the meaning behind them fell short of her comprehension of them.

"Samantha, please don't worry at this stage. It could be something very simple and easily resolved. Let's take some more blood today and a few other tests and get you some answers quickly."

Samantha thought to her beloved David. "What should I tell David?" she asked the kind Doctor.

"You should tell him exactly what I have told you. I am happy to speak to him myself, but only with your permission of course."

"No, no I will tell him," Samantha assured the doctor.

"I understand."

There was a pause as the doctor looked thoughtful.

"And Samantha, please don't concern yourself just yet. You need to concentrate on you and that baby now. Let's go through some things you need to start doing now to give yourself the best pregnancy possible."

Samantha tried to listen on as the doctor gave her detailed instructions about the next set of tests she would undergo but her words faded against the busy workings of her inner mind. Samantha could barely believe the good news when the bad news was forming over her like a storm cloud about to rain on her very joyful parade. She tried to concentrate and was thankful when the doctor began writing notes for her on a lined piece of paper. The insightful woman must have seen how difficult it was for Samantha to take all of her words in.

Leaving the office, a small bandage covering the area where the needle once more entered the vein to take the necessary samples, Samantha felt the cold as soon as she stepped onto the street. A sign perhaps that her blood pressure was heightened due to the distressing news. She stepped along the cobbled street one foot after another, not needing to think about walking as her body now compensated for the failure of her mind to act and diligently began its march for home.

As Samantha once more made her way past the Galleria Alberto Sordi, she glanced to check if the fortune teller was in residence again. With luck, he was and Samantha walked with determination to his place on the outside the old building.

"You were wrong," she spoke without introduction.

The shocked man looked up and into Samantha's reddened eyes. "I'm sorry?" He seemed unable to immediately place her face and register the contents of her words with the meaning they were presented in.

"You were wrong about not having children. I just found out I am pregnant," she explained in a little more detail her previous revelation to the fortune teller.

"I'm sorry," he replied and Samantha couldn't tell if his words were a question or an apology. He broke his glance and looked down to the cobblestones beneath his feet. Looking up again he spoke once more. "I saw no children in your future. I didn't say there were no pregnancies."

"How dare you! How could you say such a thing?"

"I can only tell you what I see and what you ask me to share."

"You are wrong!"

"I'm sorry. I wish I was."

Samantha turned away and marched once more toward her new home.

David was waiting patiently for her, greeting her at their front door as she arrived. He welcomed her home with a smile that Samantha felt obliged to return.

"Well? Any news?" he asked immediately.

She knew exactly what David's question was. He wanted to learn if they were to become parents yet. The dream that he seemed unable to wait to become a reality. Samantha didn't quite know how to tell him the news. She had barely had time to digest it herself, let alone prepare words of explanation to David. She didn't know how to tell him that they were indeed going to be parents, but that there was more yet to be uncovered about her recent poor health. How could she worry him needlessly? He didn't need that, not after everything that this man had been through in recent months.

"No news yet." Samantha chose the path of less harm and decided to hold off on telling David anything concrete until she had further information on hand.

"Oh," David was clearly disappointed. He had obviously hoped that every attempt to fall pregnant would lead to some success already. His face fell to the floor. Samantha couldn't stand to see him hurt.

"Don't worry, the doctor said sometimes these things just take a little time." She wished she could tell him. She really did but she feared telling him only half of the full story would only hurt him more down the track. She stepped into his arms and gave him a tight squeeze. She needed to remain strong right now for the both of them. She owed him that much.

Twenty

Piazza della Rotonda, Rome

The sight of the Pantheon never grew old for the loved-up couple. The view of the people milling around the famous landmark was partnered on this day with the harmonic sounds of the double bass. A sole musician had set up his temporary stage in the glow of the historic building and his playing attracted as much praise as the sights surrounding him.

David turned to Samantha to plead with her to try to eat just a bit more, "You have hardly eaten anything, my wife and this is your favourite Pasta Napoli."

"I don't know what to say. I haven't got my appetite back yet," Samantha replied.

"Do you think you might have morning sickness, all day sickness. I am not even sure what it is called."

"Who knows?" Samantha answered in the most non-committal way she could of. "I think I am just stressed about the royalty I received and worried that I may not even get enough blogs together to form anything I should be paid for."

"Well, let's pay it back. You shouldn't be feeling this stressed over money. Pay it back and then let them know when and if you finish the project but on your own timeframe. The stress of timeframes isn't helping you or your creative process."

Samantha smiled at her generous husband. How did she get so lucky as to find this man, not just once but twice in her lifetime? She reached across the table and squeezed his hand, "I will think about it." She wanted to reassure him that she would be ok and valued the lengths he would go to, to ensure she was.

David cleared his throat. It was obvious to Samantha that he had something else on his mind to declare.

"Say what you are thinking," she encouraged him.

David looked down at his own plate, all but empty of the Bolognese he had devoured in record time. An Italian favourite but a classic. He made the rumble in his throat again before finding the courage to speak.

"On our wedding day," he paused, obviously deep in thought about the words to come, "You said that I would be your last first kiss."

"Yes," Samantha added her confirmation to the fact.

"What did you mean by that?" David asked her softly.

"I meant what it sounds like, that you my darling, my husband will be the last man I ever kiss. That we are together forever."

David reached over to take the hand of the woman he loved. "And when we met again in Rome, you told me that you had known a David once."

Samantha giggled, surprised slightly by the question and the reference to her throw-away line of months earlier.

"Yes, I did. How did you remember that?"

David paused again before speaking. "I remember every detail of that night. That night changed my life forever. But I wondered if the two comments were related. That is, the last first kiss and the David that you referred to."

Samantha herself saw the link but had no idea how David had made the connection.

"I once met a boy named David. He was from Canada. I was very young, so I don't want you to be jealous. Our families were both holidaying on the Coral Coast of Fiji. His brother and him spent time playing with Sarah and I. The parents were all off doing whatever they were doing and so we would all hang out together and run around the island. We spent lots of time in the games room and swimming in the pool together."

David was listening with bated breath. "And…"

Samantha laughed nervously. "What more do you want to know?"

"How old were you?" he asked.

"Of wow, about ten years old, David was a year older and his brother was the same age as Sarah and I."

"So, you fell for an older man, even at that tender age."

Samantha giggled, "I wouldn't say that exactly. We were just kids."

"But you remember him… why?"

Samantha blushed, "A woman, always remembers her first kiss."

"In the games room?"

"Yes," Samantha giggled, "under the dart board. Not awfully romantic."

"And Sarah, did she as well have a crush with his brother?"

"Haha, yes she did as a matter of fact. She was pretty taken by him. She talked about him for years later. What was his name? I can't remember. Something starting with C or K. I should remember, the number of times I saw her scribble his name in a heart. It is going to annoy me until I remember."

"Caleb?" David suggested.

"Yes! That's it. How did you guess that?"

Samantha was impressed. David just squeezed her hand and smiled a huge smile at her.

"What is that smile about?" Samantha demanded to know.

"Give it a second," David reassured her.

Samantha stared into his confident glare. His lips turned up at the sides. His eyes held a mischievous glint to them.

"David?" she said with a questioning tone.

"One and the same," David replied.

"You are? Wait, hold on, that isn't possible. The David I met was from Canada. You are from LA."

"Not always," he assured her. "Not long after that trip, my father received a job offer in California. The whole family moved and have been there ever since. LA has always felt more home to me than Canada ever did.

"This isn't possible," Samantha struggled to digest the meaning of this latest revelation.

"That is why I stopped to talk to you in the temple at Hanoi. I looked across and saw you there. You looked exactly the same, the long dark curls, the hazel eyes, you hadn't changed a bit. I wanted to speak to you and see if it was you and if you would remember me?"

"But you never got the chance."

"Not until that night in Rome. When I saw you again, standing there in amongst that group of tourists, I knew we were meant to be. I knew straight away without a doubt that it was you."

"You have known this entire time?"

"Yep," his arrogant tone indicated a version of events he was proud to own. "So, when you mentioned the last first kiss, I thought you may had remembered as well."

Samantha threw her head back in laughter. "So, not only are you my last first kiss but you were also my first, first kiss?"

"Yep!" David was smug in his reply, "I know what I want when I see it."

The couple kissed. Not just a kiss between lovers but the kiss of soulmates destined to always be together.

The waiter approached the table to clear away the plates. "Ah young love," he swooned.

The couple broke their embrace as Samantha replied, "Ah, if only you knew!"

Twenty-One

Rome, Italy.

"Sam, that's your phone!" David bellowed from the kitchen. His hands deep into a sticky dough that he hoped would very soon become a pie. "Do you want me to get it?" he shouted into the adjourning room to Samantha who was busily clicking away on her keyboard.

"I'll get it!" she replied as she walked the short distance to her phone on the dining table. A quick glance at the caller ID indicated it was her doctor's office.

"I'll take this outside," she let David know as she swiped on the screen to answer while closing the balcony door behind her. The weather was cold still and she shivered as the cool afternoon air teased her skin.

"Samantha?" Doctor Sofia was quick to begin the conversation. "I have left you several messages already. I need you to come in and see me for your test results. We need to talk, in person."

Samantha was more than aware of the doctor's insistence to come in for an appointment. She had sensed the increased urgency in each new message and she knew without hearing the words that all was not well. She sensed it herself now. She felt not just the nausea of morning sickness, but something else too. A heaviness in her chest. A stiffness in her bones. She knew that something wasn't right and, in her mind, as long as she hadn't had the bad news confirmed, she could live with it being a mere thought in her overactive imagination.

"Samantha. I don't want to say this, but if you refuse to come in, you leave me with no choice but to contact David myself. You can't ignore what I need to speak to you about."

"No!" Samantha was quick to respond. "Don't tell David. I will do that myself. Just tell me when and I will come in."

"Tomorrow morning at ten a.m. And Samantha do not cancel on me. I will see you tomorrow and if I don't, I will be ringing David. Please think about bringing him with you this time. I would prefer to speak to the both of you."

"I will be there," Samantha promised.

Returning to the warmth of their cosy apartment, David sensed something wasn't right.

"Who was that?"

"Just Sedgwick," Samantha lied. He was ringing to update me on his latest little adventures.

"You didn't speak for long," David challenged her story.

"You know him. Fickle as ever. He saw someone he needed to speak to and had to go."

"Oh?" David sensed more to the call than what Samantha was letting on.

* * *

The following morning as promised, Samantha made the short journey to Doctor Sofia's office. She was welcomed by the friendly receptionist by name and shown into the dark, mahogany wood furnished office. The doctor appeared surprised by her appearance but pleased to finally have the chance to discuss the test results face to face.

"Thank you for coming in Samantha," Sofia began.

"I didn't feel I had a choice," Samantha replied.

"I am sorry for that. You left me little options when you didn't return any of my calls."

"I am keen to now hear the results. Let's get this over with shall we."

"I understand," the doctor agreed. "Samantha, the test results have shown the presence of cancer."

A long pause followed to allow the words to sink in.

"We need more tests and I can't confirm until those results come through but what it appears to so far indicate is lung cancer that could, if untreated become metastatic to bone.

Samantha sat still, her face blank, not yet indicating the seriousness of the information being imparted to her.

"And treatment?"

The doctor looked to the floor first and then to Samantha. She simply grimaced and shook her head. "We need to get specialists involved immediately. If we leave it much longer, we may only have the option of palliative care."

"The baby?" Samantha barely held it together long enough to allow the words to flow from her mouth.

"It is too early in the pregnancy for us to have any options for a full-term pregnancy right now."

Samantha's bottom lip quivered as her hand reached down to her stomach.

"Our baby."

Twenty-Two

Rome, Italy

Samantha packed with haste. There were few possessions she needed to take on this journey. Her laptop, camera, passport and a few items of light clothing. She hoped she might miss him altogether, she planned for it as she threw the last few items into her carry-on luggage. The door of the apartment closed as his voice echoed through the small apartment. He was early. Home early from the tour of the Vatican.

"I'm home, where is my beautiful wife?" he yelled into the apartment as he walked through the doorway to the bedroom. As he caught a glimpse of her bag, he stopped on the spot.

"Where are you going?"

"You were right. I need to give back the royalty money. The pressure to write the blogs is too much for me right now. My health and everything is being affected by the stress of getting everything done to their deadline. I hope it is still ok to do so."

"Of course, Sam." David looked relieved to hear that Samantha had made the decision to put her publishing dreams on hold for the time being at least. The pressure it had placed on her wasn't good for her or for her health.

"Just give me a minute to throw some things into a bag and ring and have someone take tomorrow's tour for me.

"No," Samantha spat out, more aggressively than she had probably meant to. "I mean, this is something I need to do on my own."

"You are going to London on your own?"

David appeared perplexed. He couldn't quite comprehend why Samantha needed to do this on her own.

"Yes."

"Let's make a trip of it together. Make more memories. More pins on our map of places in the world, we have made love."

"Please," she begged of him. "I am just making a quick trip, there and back. I just want to tell them in person that I am breaking contract, deal with the consequences and fly home again."

There was nothing left for David to barter with. "OK, if you are sure," he conceded defeat. "How long will you be gone for?"

"I don't know," Samantha replied.

Every instinct in his body told him something wasn't right. Samantha's concise answers, not out of anger but with a certain firmness that didn't fit with the scenario.

"Let me at least take you to the airport. Give you a proper farewell kiss. I will miss my wife while she is gone."

"Don't be stupid David. That is a waste of money and your time. I am perfectly fine to do this on my own. And besides a night or two apart won't kill us."

"Yes, it will," David replied sheepishly. "I will miss you every second we are apart. Are you sure I can't come with you?"

Samantha looked in the eyes of the man she loved for the first time since he entered their bedroom. "You are right. I am sorry. I will miss you too my husband."

Within moments, Samantha was out of the door and in the private car taking her directly and without delay to the Leonardo da Vinci International Airport.

David watched Samantha walk out of the door before he stepped on to the balcony to wave her goodbye. She didn't look up. She jumped into the car without even glancing skyward to see her husband wave goodbye from their second-storey apartment. Something wasn't right. David could sense it in every part of his being. This wasn't his Samantha. Something more than just the publishing obligations was bothering her.

He walked back inside and picked up his phone. He dialed the number and let it ring until it went to messagebank. He opened his mouth to speak, to leave a message for the recipient to call him back. But he didn't. He hung up the phone and placed his mobile back on the dining table.

He desperately needed to know more and feared the one person that might have the information he needed was Doctor Sofia, but he couldn't betray Samantha's confidence. He would just have to rely on his wife to tell him what was wrong when she was ready in her own time to do so.

* * *

The Roman airport was busy for an ordinary day of the week. Samantha enjoyed getting lost in the chaos of international travel. People coming and going, tearful send-offs, gleeful reunions. The anticipation of adventure and the unknown in the air. But Samantha's destination wasn't one full of the mysterious unknown. The country of her destination was one she was quite familiar with. From the long stretching coastline, the fragrant foods and the warm balmy weather, Vietnam was well known to Samantha. A fitting final destination to spend the last of her days.

A tribute as such to her chance meeting once more with the soulmate she had recently learnt to be one in the same as the young David she shared her very first kiss with. Hanoi, the place of the Temple of the Horse. The place she said a prayer to her beloved father and sister, the same place that David found her, all those years after their very first meeting.

Hanoi was the place she would call home as the cancer that destroyed her future would take hold on her body.

184

Twenty-Three

Rome, Italy

"Please Sofia, I beg of you. Tell me whatever you can. I understand your obligations to Samantha but I am worried about her safety. I haven't heard from her in two days. I expected her home already. I can't reach her. She isn't returning my calls. Please, I need to know what you told her. Is there some reason why she might have taken off on her own like this?"

"David, I wish I could help. I can't tell you anything more at this stage. You have to be patient. I am sure she will return and tell you everything herself."

"So, there is something to tell?"

"David, please don't ask anymore of me than I can give."

"And if she doesn't come back?"

"I don't know what to tell you. I am truly sorry."

Twenty-Four

Halong Bay, Vietnam

Sailing slowly into Halong Bay, Samantha tried to visualise what the mesmerising wonder of the world would look like by air. Locals believed that the limestone formations were created by a fiery dragon who upon witnessing their enemies attack, descended from heaven to build a fortress to protect its people. Spurting streams of jade droplets from its mouth into the water, the dragon was said to have created no fewer than 1969 individual pieces of landscape. The overall masterpiece had proven too much for the enemy sailors inexperienced in the stretch of water, their vessels soon falling prey to the jagged shorelines. The treacherous formations had saved the country and its people from invasion.

1969 was an important number for another reason. It was the year the Vietnamese people's beloved President Ho Chi Ming died. Samantha couldn't help but wonder at the coincidence of this special number as the small wooden junk moved steadily further into the rocky safeguard.

The insignificant green foliage of the trees were dwarfed by the gigantic structures, scattered haphazardly through the dark emerald waters of this bay of natural beauty. The place of magnificence helped to ground Samantha. The structures, the history and the massive size of the bay made her feel insignificant in comparison. This place felt as foreign and as far away from her life in Rome as she could plausibly get.

She turned to the glowing red light on the horizon. It was sunrise in Halong Bay. It was if the ancient descending dragon, said to be living peacefully in the bay had nudged her awake to bask in its amazing glory. She moved steadily around her small cabin to find her camera among the debris that was the remnants of her small backpack.

Making her way silently to the balcony at the stern of the wooden junk she tried to move quietly and quickly so as not to wake her neighbours with heavy footsteps on the creaky panelled floor.

Hardly taking time to focus for fear of losing the gorgeous light display, Samantha raised her camera and clicked. First time worked a charm and there it was captured forever, her very own five a.m. morning sunrise in Halong Bay. She rushed back inside to find her laptop. The universe was giving her yet another wonderful opportunity, the chance to practice her descriptive writing; the area she had known to be her greatest weakness in her newly found craft of memoir writing. Her new hobby was a welcome distraction from her constant thoughts of dying.

For the vast number of tourist boats in the bay, there was not a sound beside the distant chirping of the small birds that found shelter in the hidden caves among the bay. The low hum of the generator barely registered in her consciousness as it was her constant companion all night. The junk had somehow managed to turn to face the sunset, her cabin at the corner rear of the vessel gained uninterrupted views. Samantha had a front row seat to one of the most unspoiled natural wonders of the world.

The water was still, barely a ripple as just the faintest sea breeze softly skimmed her already warm skin. The boat turned once more, just ever so slightly to offer a perfect photo opportunity. She framed the gigantic limestone formation in the old wooden frame of the boat window. The glass panelling for some reason didn't want to stay put and she found herself trying to use her legs to hold it in place for a natural landscape photo.

She maneuvered on the bed, twisting one-way and then another to get just the right angle. Finally, she gave in and let the window have its way as the star in her photographic attempt at majesty. She pointed and clicked and paused to check out the latest attempt. Her legs ached from the small exertion that was the entirety of all of her physical exercise from the last two days on the wooden boat.

Her resignation to her fate had proven its usefulness as without this time to reflect on her own, she would have never visited the bay. The photo of the sunrise was perfect.

"This is amazing," she uttered to the audience of two. She wondered what it was that woke her at just the perfect minute to capture this most incredible moment in time. Was this sunrise the most incredible sunrise or did the limited number of sunrises left give this particular one a sort of mystical sense of importance?

Thinking more and more of the mythical dragon that had created these jagged formations, she wondered briefly about calling this latest work, Rising Dragon. Although she continued to write she doubted if she would ever again publish. Writing now was just a distraction from the inevitable end to her life.

A sense of calm washed over her. For the time being she felt untouchable, absolutely protected and safe from all harm within the parameter of the limestone fortress. Her mind as it did often, leapt forward to her departure already with a sense of regret that she would be leaving this magical, mythical venue within a few hours. She stopped herself from forward thinking as was her current practice and brought herself back to the present. She brought herself back to the here and now and back to the moment in time that she would remember for the rest of her short life.

The sun peeped back around the headland, sending a piercing hot ray of light into her cabin. She made the decision to skip the tourist activities for the morning, the tai chi and the kayaking, to stay put for the few hours she had left in her own peaceful, gorgeous little paradise.

She laid on her bed, her laptop rested on bent knees, a new position for writing for her but it felt good for this time of the morning. It was luxurious to be able to enjoy a lazy morning looking out onto the stunning view from her bed. She stretched across the smooth white linen sheet for her camera. She found it and turned her head to aim directly at the orange light reflecting from her windowsill. Last photo, she promised herself knowing full well she wouldn't be able to live up to it.

She thought once more of the title, Rising Dragon, the legend of the dragon coming to the innocent people of Vietnam to protect them from their enemies as the story was told to her. She wondered how she might conjure up her own rising dragon when she needed it the most. She wondered also if the dragon is a metaphor for courage. A courage, which lately seemed to have failed her, or abandoned her altogether.

The Vietnamese people paid homage to four sacred creatures. They are the dragon, which of course would be given its great importance in saving its people during wartime attack. There was also the phoenix, the unicorn and finally the humble turtle. She looked down at the silver turtle that adorned her left foot. A tribute to the friendly turtles she swam with in Bora Bora. She wondered if this turtle could be her lucky charm and then she remembered that all of her luck had already run out.

She stretched to ponder her luck for a moment as the dark shadow of a new bruise on the inside of her left arm caught her eye. She did a quick stocktake of injuries to date. Twenty nights in Vietnam and she had only one bruise, one small cut on the outside of her small finger on her right hand and a smallish but deep enough gash to her right palm. Not bad for her. She found a solid piece of wood and knocked three times so as not to unsettle her good fortune to date.

Superstition had it that when you are feeling lucky and actually think it or say it out loud, knocking on wood three times prevents it from escaping. The other story she had heard about this, was that knocking three times prevents evil spirits from coming through a virtual doorway that you open up when you have these thoughts. If left opened, these evil spirits are able to come through and take your good fortune away. This sounded far too ominous for her, so she decided to stick with the first theory. She didn't need any more bad luck than she had already been dealt.

She felt a flutter in her stomach and placed her hand over her unborn baby.

"Good morning little one. Hang in there, won't you."

Samantha closed her eyes and said a silent prayer for her child. She pleaded with the rising dragon that she was sure was watching over her that day.

"Please, keep me alive just long enough for him to be born."

Twenty-Five

Los Angeles, California

"Stop pacing for God's sake, that is not helping," Caleb yelled at his brother. "You are not being productive when you are this wound up."

"What do you suggest I do?" David replied back.

"Anything but that. Just sit, sit for a second and tell me again from the start. What happened in the days leading up to her trip to London?"

"She was distant, not herself. Not happy. Shut off. She obviously had something on her mind that she didn't feel she could share. But I don't understand. I don't know what could have been so serious that she couldn't share with me."

"And the doctor won't tell you anything?"

"No, not yet. I think she is caving. She seems to be concerned as well. I am phoning her every day to see what she will share, but so far it is just vague references to Samantha having some things to work out for herself."

"Ah!" Caleb let out a sigh.

"There has to be more we can do." David shot up from his seated position once more. "I can't just sit here and do nothing."

"What are the authorities saying?" Caleb enquired.

"They won't tell me anything. I am not legally her husband remember. As far as they are concerned, I am the jilted lover and no one will give me any information. I can't even find out if she actually flew to London. The publishers won't take my calls. They won't confirm or deny any meeting with Samantha. I have no idea what to do next."

"How far are you willing to go to find her?" Caleb had an idea brewing.

"Anything, I will do anything," David reassured his brother.

"Even if it means breaking laws and privacy?"

"I have nothing to lose at this stage."

"OK, pass me my laptop. Let's do some hacking."

"Is that what you really do for a living?" David asked his brother.

"Let's just say that I offer my business clients an all-round service. And it's not that difficult really. People would be shocked to learn how easy it is to find personal information they might not want the world to know. Now let's find your Samantha."

Twenty-Six

Hanoi, Vietnam

Samantha checked-in to the modest, family run hotel that would be her home for the coming weeks.

"Welcome back Samantha!"

The hotel manager and eldest son of the business-minded family ran to greet his much-anticipated guest. "I am so happy to see you again. How long has it been?"

"A year and a half already Kevin," Samantha informed him. "I had hoped you would still be here. I was surprised you remembered me when I called."

"How could I forget you. The improvements you made to the website has seen our little hotel booming. Do you think you would have time to look at another one for our newest hotel? Your English is so much better than mine."

"Your English is perfect, Kevin. I dare say it just comes more naturally for me as it is the only language I speak.

"I am more than happy to make the same deal as last time. You stay for as long as you want, free of charge, if you can help with some bits and pieces of writing for us."

"I would be honoured to help, Kevin but I am more than happy to pay my own way."

"My mother would not hear of it. She will be most pleased to see you again. How long do you think you will stay this time?"

"I'm not sure yet."

The hesitation in Samantha's voice didn't go unnoticed by her familiar host.

"Something is not right is it?"

"I have just been a bit unwell of late," was all that Samantha wanted to disclose.

"Have a lychee, fresh from our family farm."

"Are lychees your answer for every problem?" Samantha joked with her friend.

"Hungry? Eat lychee. Thirsty? Eat lychee. Tired? Eat lychee," Kevin joked

"Lose weight? Eat lychee… yes, yes I remember well," Samantha teased back. "If it is ok with you, I might grab my key."

Kevin handed over the key to Samantha's favourite room and the only one in the hotel with a private balcony. He carried her small bag up the flight of concrete steps and opened the door to the humble dwelling. She walked to the balcony and flung open the glass door to allow the hot air to blow through. Samantha loved sitting and watching the busy comings and goings of Hanoi below her. She intended to write as much as she could in the time she had left. Writing her thoughts, her history and her epic love story for the child she hoped she could carry to full-term or near enough for a successful delivery. Knowing she wouldn't get to see her beloved child grow, she wanted to capture as much as she could in writing to leave behind for him and for his father.

A tear fell as she thought of David and imagined the pain he must be going through with her sudden and unexplained departure. She imagined Doctor Sofia had told David already the bad news. She knew she should contact him soon to let him know that she was ok for now and that she hoped to hang on long enough for him to meet his son.

"Please tell me what is wrong Samantha," Kevin begged her.

Kevin hesitated.

"There is nothing in the world, that is bad enough that it can't be shared amongst friends."

"Thank you. You truly are a good friend. I promise I will share with you. I just need some rest first. I am tired from my travels and this heat. I forgot just how hot your homeland gets."

"You didn't just do that, did you?"

"What?"

"Try to pawn me off with talk of the weather." Kevin began making for the door. "I give you until tomorrow to talk and then I am calling mother."

Samantha cringed.

"Yes. Mother will get you talking," Kevin promised as he walked out of the door, closing it gently behind him.

Samantha walked over and glanced at her phone. She knew there would be no messages for the freshly purchased sim card guaranteed no one could contact her. That didn't stop her social media notifications from blowing up into the hundreds. Every person she knew must have left a message for her. She had no doubt that David was busily contacting them all to try to find her. She didn't have the strength yet to reply, not to them nor to David. Not just yet. She needed more time to process her death before she could let anyone else in.

Finding the remote control for the ancient air-conditioning unit, Samantha pressed the red button hoping to hear the whirl of the vents open to expel the cool air into her stifling hot room. Nothing happened. She tried again and again, no action was forthcoming. She picked up the hotel phone to ring Kevin.

"Hello Ms Samantha?" his chipper voice sing-songed through the phone.

"Kevin, I don't think the air-conditioning unit is working. I can't seem to turn it on."

"So sorry, I will have someone come and look at it tomorrow. In the meantime, if you are hot… eat lychee. I will send you a plate full."

Samantha giggled at the inspirational hospitality and belief that this sacred fruit of the family farm was the tonic to all of life's woes. She thanked Kevin and replaced the phone piece in its cradle. Curious, she googled the health benefits of eating lychees. Not surprisingly, they were well documented. She read the health information on various websites, all confirming Kevin's theories that lychees did indeed possess potential health benefits.

Samantha read her findings out loud to the empty room. "Lychee contains a good amount of antioxidant, Vitamin C and Vitamin B. Lychee is a rich source of nutrient that is required for the production of blood."

Samantha wondered if there was a natural food source, plant or otherwise that had been reported to cure cancer. She could only wish. She kept reading. It couldn't hurt to do some research on the topic.

After a period of vivacious reading, Samantha picked up the phone one more time.

"Hello, Ms Samantha," Kevin answered again, "How can I help you? Are you ready to talk yet?"

"Kevin, when did you say your mother was next around? I would like to talk to her about something. And you are right, there is no more time to waste. I need her help."

"Of course, I will ring her now. She can come in from the farm in the morning. She will be happy to see you."

***

"David!" Caleb yelled at his brother from the other room. "Bring me another scotch and one for yourself. I think I have found something."

"What?" David asked as he peered his head around the door from the adjoining room. "Did you find her?"

"Not yet, but I think we are getting closer."

David joined his brother in the office of their family home as he handed him a refill of their father's favourite scotch.

"I found on her credit card that she bought an airline ticket, but I can't tell where to. It was more than the cost of simply flying to London, but that doesn't really help as she could be anywhere. And from what you have said, she is an experienced traveller, so she literally could have flown into any country in the world," Caleb added.

"What passport is she travelling on?" Caleb continued.

"Australian, but the embassy has been less than helpful. I'm not family, not even her legal husband, so they won't even hear me out. Her friends know nothing at all or if they do, they are choosing not to tell me. I have contacted everyone I can locate. They are all saying they haven't heard from her."

"Ok, so let's try another angle, but I'm not sure if it is relevant or even helpful."

"Go on," David encouraged.

Caleb began again, "Travelling on an Australian passport, she wouldn't require visas for too many countries, would she?"

"Most countries would be visa free or visa on arrival. Some middle eastern countries, might require a visa application. Russia possibly. Why? What are you thinking?"

"I can't tell too much, but there does seem to be a payment here for what looks to be an e-visa. Do you know why she would need that?"

A smile shot across David's face. "I know exactly where she is. A country she knows and loves and one of the few places she would visit which requires an Australian to obtain a visa. She is in Vietnam."

"Vietnam is a large place David. I don't think that is going to help you much."

"You are a genius little brother. I know exactly where I can find her. Click on that site, Caleb and order me an e-visa for Vietnam and a flight while you are at it. I am ringing Doctor Sofia one last time, to see if she will now tell me exactly what she told Samantha before she left.

Twenty-Seven

Temple of the Horse, Hanoi, Old Quarter.

David waited patiently for Samantha to arrive. He had prepared to camp out day and night trusting that eventually she would appear at the Temple of the Horse. The place they found each other once more after years apart. He knew in his soul that Samantha had returned to Vietnam. A country she knew well and loved. He was determined that he would not leave Hanoi without her.

He stood staring at the grey horse that enjoyed centre stage of the small temple. The eyes stared back at him, watching him in a knowing fashion. It truly was as if the statue of the horse was alive. There was a presence about it. This was the exact spot that he had found his Samantha over twelve months ago. And to think that he had lost her again in just a fleeting moment. This had to be the place. This had to be where he would find her again. A peace that he hadn't felt in weeks, filled his soul. He suddenly felt her close.

"David, what happens when you die?" Samantha's soft voice echoed through the silence.

He turned around to see her, a mere few steps behind him. He rushed to her and grabbed her into his embrace. His intuition had been correct. He knew she would come once more to the temple. He squeezed her tightly as the words she spoke filled his head. He knew everything now. He knew about the cancer and about their child. He knew that the chances of her making a full recovery were slim but he refused to believe them. He needed his soulmate in his life. He refused to believe he would go on without his wife and his child beside him.

"Sam, that's not what's happening to you. I don't want to hear you speak of death."

"David, I need to. We need to have this conversation."

David sighed. He couldn't think of Samantha not growing old with him. He searched for some words of encouragement. He understood that indeed they needed to have the conversation around her illness.

"You live on. Your energy, your essence, your soul lives in another place."

"Where?"

"I don't know."

"Then how can you be so sure?'

"Because I can. I know that my father left to be with my mother. I know he found her wherever she was. I trust that they found Sarah too. They met her too, you know, all those years ago. Maybe their meeting was for some higher purpose. Maybe it was so they could keep an eye on her. Watch over her like a daughter wherever they are all together now. I am sure your father found Sarah as well. I am sure she is being cared for by people who love her."

"Will you find me?"

"Of course, I will find you, my wife." David leant down and kissed Samantha on the forehead.

"How will you know it is me? We might not look like this. We might have different names."

"I will know from your kiss."

She giggled for a moment. The relief at being back in David's arms was immense.

"So, you go around kissing random women until you find me? I don't like the sound of that."

"I will kiss only one and that one will be you. Trust me Samantha, I found you not once or twice, but three times on this earth. I will find you again. I won't stop until I do!"

Samantha's eyes closed. His promise gave her the reassurance she needed.

"And I will find you too, my baby boy." He leant forward and placed a tender kiss on the growing stomach that sheltered his unborn child.

"I couldn't stay. I couldn't stay and risk the chance that they did anything to harm our baby. I just knew what was coming next, talk of radiation, of chemotherapy. None of which our baby boy could live through. I wanted to keep him safe. I needed to stay alive long enough to give you your son."

"I know."

"David? Why are you here?"

"How could I not be?" he replied.

"But?" She didn't know what else to say.

She looked into his eyes and was simply grateful for his company. The pain in her body was becoming unbearable. She felt weak and exhausted and needed her husband's strong arms around her.

David took her hand and kissed it gently. He looked into her eyes. "Samantha, I have known you in my soul for years. I have loved you since our first kiss."

She couldn't hear any more. She didn't want to believe that her life with David was to come to such a sudden end.

"David, I'm tired."

He leaned down and kissed her forehead. He knew exactly what to say. "I understand. Let's get you home. You need your rest to get better. And you will get better," he promised.

His words sounded like a solemn declaration from his soul to hers. She felt hopeful for a moment. She realised that the doctor had told him everything, yet he believed they would survive this together.

"I want to stay here in Vietnam."

As difficult as it was to tell him, he deserved to be a part of her plan too. He deserved to journey with her and she needed him to be there with her.

"I have an idea I want to try. We have nothing to lose by trying some alternative medicines. Do you feel like a trip to the Mekong Delta with me?"

"Anything for you," David assured her.

The pair stood in each other's arms. Inside the temple, they experienced another moment. A moment of promising their love to one another, not just in this lifetime, but for eternity, as their souls find each other long after their bodies have left their earthly home for whatever realm they venture to. The couple stood enveloped in each other. Silent for a long while.

"David, I am sorry I left. I panicked. I didn't know how to tell you. After everything, I couldn't tell you. I knew I could with some time and distance. I just needed some time to sort some things through in my head before I shared the terrible news with you."

"Hey, we don't work within the construct of time remember? For us it is all about moments and memories. Time can kiss my butt. She is not my mistress."

He paused. "And together, we are going to show her, she no longer controls us."

"Yeah, you are right. Time can't tell us when we are through. We ditched that bitch long ago. Moments and memories," Samantha agreed.

The pair smiled at each other. It felt good to both of them to be in this battle together. They were a formidable force once joined.

"I love you," Samantha uttered.

"I love you more than you could ever imagine," David replied.

Twenty-Eight

Mekong Delta, Vietnam

Life in Vietnam for the pair consisted of a series of inspiring highs followed by devasting lows. It seemed every healer they spoke to offered different thoughts on how to cure Samantha. Many swore by their natural remedies. Ancient practices had been touted and experimented with throughout the history of their country. It was difficult for the couple to know how far to take each avenue before moving onto something new to try.

Samantha's least favourite of all the techniques had been the blood-letting. Using the traditional method of leeches to draw the blood, Samantha was forced to lay still on her stomach as the small worms were placed with care onto her back. And David had been there holding her hand for every minute of the gruelling treatment. As a food was offered as the miracle cure, David was beside Samantha indulging in every bite alongside her.

It was with trepidation that the couple consumed the infamous snake wine. So vile was its taste that Samantha nearly regurgitated the entire mouthful before she had time to swallow. She watched with sympathy as David's eyes went a shade of bloodshot red as he forced his body to absorb the pungent yellow coloured liquid. So potent was the batch, only a few millilitres were required at regular intervals to work its magic. Samantha was unsure she could continue past the first glass.

"You don't have to do this one with me. I wouldn't wish that on anybody. I don't need you to endure this as well."

David stood his ground. He was part of the treatment plan. He was prepared to accept any fate the healers recommended if it held any chance at all that Samantha could be helped.

"I am with you my wife. Together, the two of us. I'm not leaving you to do this on your own."

"How are you feeling?" David asked as Samantha grimaced at the taste of the following glass of the snake fermented medicinal wine.

"If that didn't chase the cancer cells from my body, nothing will."

Samantha thought of her child having to undergo everything she was, "Sorry little dude, I hope you didn't get much of that." She placed her hand on her now protruding stomach. So far so good. Although the symptoms of the cancer hadn't dissipated, she was still alive and the pregnancy had progressed through its first trimester. "Hang in there little one. Mummy and Daddy are trying everything we can."

David walked to place his hand on her stomach. "Is he ok?" he asked with concern for his wife and child.

"He's a strong little boy. Just like his father. He is doing ok in there."

"So, you do think he is a he?"

"I have a feeling, it's a boy, but let's wait to find out for sure. If that is ok with you? I want to wait and with any luck meet him for myself for the first time when he arrives."

"That sounds very hopeful." David smiled at the thought of the day he would meet his first-born child.

"Well, we have to stay positive, don't we? I swear I couldn't keep doing any of this if I didn't hold onto at least a little hope that it was working."

"It's going to work Sam. It will. There is no other choice."

Sitting on the deck of their rented boat on the Mekong Delta, David and Samantha sat hand in hand looking over the impressive waterway. A ripple in the water caught their attention. A snake, its head reared glided effortlessly across the surface of the water. David jumped up from his chair and turned to Samantha,

"Should I jump in and grab it for you? Dinner maybe?" he laughed.

Samantha roared with laughter. "I dare you!"

"I'll do it," David joked as he made his way to the side of the boat, arms raised above his head as if to dive into the water below.

The couple laughed, as much as a release of the months of built up tension as to the ridiculousness of the situation they found themselves in. Sitting about a rickety wooden boat on the most famous river in Vietnam as they moved from one location to the next sampling ancient medicinal cures.

Samantha stopped laughing as her hand fell to her stomach. Her astonished face turned to David. "He kicked."

David ran to her side. He placed his palm on her belly and waited for another movement.

"I felt it," he yelled. "Hello little man. This is your Dad."

Samantha's eyes watered. Pure joy filtered through every cell in her body. "He is ok. He is ok in there," she said to assure both herself and her husband.

"I knew he would be. He's our boy. He is being strong just like his mother."

"There he goes again."

"We have ourselves a little gridiron player. What age can we sign him up?"

"Gridiron? No way, this one is playing rugby league, just like his grandfather."

"Remember that rugby match your father organised in Fiji? Local versus tourist. My father got hammered by some hundred-kilogram local. He talked about that for years."

"The tourists didn't stand a chance. Remember, all of us kids running the sidelines cheering our Dads on."

"How did they ever think up such an idea?"

"Our dads did well, didn't they? Well your father was a little bit hopeless," Samantha added. "No offence of course."

David laughed, "Dad didn't even know what rugby was, let alone what the rules were."

The pair smiled at the memory.

"I wish they were both here now. Our fathers."

"They are. Trust me. They are watching over us," David reassured her.

Samantha looked skyward to shout her demands to their fathers, "Then send us the bloody cure already, won't you!"

David's chest caught at the sudden thought of his Samantha up there with them. He banished the thought from his mind. As much as he held hope that Samantha would get better soon, the fear that she wouldn't was never too far from his mind.

Days had passed before they were ready to venture onto their next meeting. The village elder and respected healer took his time listening to the symptoms Samantha rattled off. Both were surprised when he suggested a blood test. No other healer had yet combined both the ancient methods with the more conventional and modern techniques they had been used to. They took a moment to answer the man.

"Is there a problem with that?" he asked them.

"What are you looking for?" David asked him.

"I need to know more about what I am treating. Our traditional methods are not in dispute with modern medicine but instead work in conjunction with our advancements in technology and understanding. If you don't mind, I would also like to see scans of your lungs."

"Yes, yes of course. Whatever you need," David didn't hesitate to assure the elder. "Do you actually think you can help my wife?"

The elder's mouth formed a smile. "I have helped many and I will do everything to help both your wife and your child."

David stood to walk toward the elderly medicine man. He grabbed his hand between his palms and shook it. "Thank you, doctor."

"I cannot use the term doctor, nor would I even if I could. You can simply call me Phuc."

"Thank you Phuc," David said as he shook the man's hand again.

When they returned to the healer again, results already confirmed to be on hand at the office, both were feeling optimistic about the future treatment. They waited no time at all before they were ushered into the office. David immediately began by asking the elder for his thoughts on a plan moving forward.

"Well, it doesn't appear as dire as I had first imagined," Phuc explained to them.

"Really?" Samantha asked with a hopeful tone.

"Don't misunderstand me. There are cancerous cells in your lungs, but I believe them to be isolated to the lungs and no further.

From what I can see that is. I cannot guarantee this to be one hundred percent true."

The couple clasped hands and squeezed tightly. Their hopes raised that they had made the right decision to seek alternative means to fight the disease.

"So now I want you to try a chemo-therapy of sorts. Similar to what you would have received back in Rome, but instead of a chemically manufactured drug, we are going to use naturally produced materials. We want to alter the make-up of your body, so unfortunately, I want to try blood-letting with you. I know you didn't like it but no leeches this time, just needles. We want to harvest some of your own plasma to inject back into your system. The body actually heals itself and with a bit of a helping hand from us, it can cure itself as well."

"I will do anything you suggest Phuc," Samantha readily agreed.

"And I want to add some of the centuries-old techniques, you might not have tried as yet. One of those would be to drink snake blood.

David and Samantha turned to each other. They smiled and squeezed their combined hands again.

"I'm with you every step, my wife."

"You better be," Samantha smiled as she replied to her husband.

Phuc continued with his explanation, "I want you to be aware that you may start to feel worse before you get better. We are trying to shock your system into a radical overhaul so you will have to trust me and keep your faith."

"We will," the couple said in unison.

Twenty-Nine

Ho Chi Minh City, Vietnam

"David, I just can't do this anymore," Samantha pleaded as David rubbed her back. "I can't stand the nausea. All of this must be hurting the baby."

"I'm here. We will get through this. Just a little while longer and the worst of it should have passed."

"I'm sorry I couldn't save him." Samantha let the tears flow down her face.

Days had passed quickly now with little progress as far as the couple could see. Samantha mainly slept and when she wasn't sleeping, she was throwing up. She had never felt as sick in all her life.

David tried to remain strong, never speaking his fears out loud. He stayed positive and attentive, never leaving his Samantha's side. As a torrential rain fell to bring some much-needed relief to the warm and humid day, the couple fell asleep once more in each other's arms.

Samantha woke in the dead of night to turn to David sleeping beside her. David's hand was enclosed in her right palm. She knew now was the time to say goodbye. The pain was too much and she didn't want to hurt the people she loved any more than she already had.

The medicinal solutions that sprung forth in their search for a remedy hadn't had the immediate effect the pair had hoped for. Samantha had been insistent on staying in Vietnam knowing that the humidity made the pain just that slightly more bearable. A return to a still cold of Italy would cause avoidable aches. Plus, she feared it was too late in her illness to make the long flight back to David's adopted home.

Her body was weary and exhausted. She felt her eyes drift shut again. She used what little strength she had to force them open. She looked at her sleeping David next to her. Not leaving her alone for even the briefest amounts of time. He too was exhausted but forever hopeful. With great confidence, he promised her daily that they would beat the battle her body was fighting against the disease. He was her beacon of hope. Her greatest regret would be that their son, would no doubt die with her and never meet his loving father.

As Samantha's eyes grew tired, she realised she would have to close them soon for good. She began to search the words for her final goodbye.

"David…" she began, stopping suddenly knowing there were no words left to speak.

"Samantha." David opened his eyes, awake at the mere sound of her voice. "Save your strength my darling, there is nothing you need to say right now. We have plenty of moments left, don't fear. This is not goodbye. Don't say goodbye to me yet."

The sides of Samantha's mouth curled into a smile. "Kiss me," she smirked as she gave the instruction.

David leaned over and paused ever so quickly before he placed his lips on hers.

The sensual feel of his mouth on hers excited Samantha's weary body. The tingling sensation that she felt the moment he touched her for the very first time was still there, not diminished by repetition nor familiarity. They both relished every second of the tender moment, for both secretly harboured the fear it would be their last.

David had been there nearly her whole life. Her soulmate embodied in a person who would journey with her from a distance.

It wasn't the amount of time they had spent together, but that they knew each other's souls.

In the end, Samantha could look back on a life well lived and a loving man who was the embodiment of the beautiful statue of Michelangelo's David. Their love story would be remembered by moments and a promise to always find each other.

Samantha closed her eyes again.

Thirty

Paris, France

The funeral was a packed affair. The old church full of people who were family, and friends, who had become family. Each making the trip to say their farewells in David and Samantha's much-loved adopted home in the city of Paris. With the end so quick, most didn't get the chance to say their goodbyes in person and needed this day to pay their respects to their beloved friend.

The guest of honour, stood before the grieving crowd to utter just a few words. None were strangers, the room was packed with loved ones. The guests were there not just for themselves but for each other.

The elderly speaker trembled at the podium and began to talk. The room fell silent.

"It is difficult for me to find the words to describe how I feel today, I wish I had been a better writer and could have prepared something to say to you all." Samantha hesitated for just a moment. She took a deep breath in to regain the courage to continue. She opened her mouth to speak but no words came out.

Samantha paused again. Her tears flowed past her sunken cheeks. Her face aged with time, she was pale and weak, as if she had lost the will to continue.

"Today I bury my soulmate. I loved him more than he could have ever imagined. Without him journeying beside me I don't know how I go on." She could barely continue. She bowed her head, took a deep breath and thought of David. She had to find the words to say what she needed to say. She had to find the strength to go on.

She glanced out to the quiet crowd to find the face of her only son, Sebastian Phuc. His middle name given in honour of the caring healer who saved his and Samantha's lives. Taking centre place in the front pew of the old Parisian church he was surrounded by his four younger sisters. Aged now themselves, they held tightly onto each other's hands. Her grandchildren and great grandchildren occupied the three rows behind them. Tears from the youngest, were comforted by the eldest amongst the children. Samantha stared into the eyes of her son, he had David's green-brown eyes. He smiled at her and encouraged his mother to continue.

"Sixty-fours years ago, when I thought I would die I said my goodbyes to my husband and my son. I now feel ashamed to say that I had lost all hope of recovery, but not David. I had given up on myself and on my son. I didn't think either of us would make it through the night. But David never gave up on us. He promised me we would share this life together. A house full of love and many, many, children and grandchildren. That is what he wanted, and I think I gave him that." Samantha smiled at her enormous family before her.

The members of the audience chuckled as they looked at the large, loving family David and Samantha had created together.

"Our life is the material for the greatest romance story ever told. My first love, my only love, meeting as children, finding each other in the world not once, nor twice but three times. And once the love of my life walked back into my world that fateful night in Rome, over six decades ago, I was certain of one thing and one thing only, I was never letting him go again."

"To say we were soulmates, feels like an understatement for I knew David long before I ever met him. If I believe in anything, I believe that we are old souls, that we have journeyed through lives before this one and I know we will meet again one day."

Samantha paused. She missed her David with every ounce of her being. She had but a few more words to say. She owed him every moment of it.

"Time is the ultimate leveller. Time is the only commodity that cannot be traded, bargained for, given or received. Time is all we have my dear friends. Time to create the memories with our loved ones. And David and I once we were given a second chance, we didn't waste a precious hour of our time together."

"We counted our life not by days but by the moments we shared. At ninety-nine years of age, David was certain he would make one hundred. He missed his goal by only a few short months. He promised me to make the mark for us both. And there isn't anything that is going to stop me from doing just that… for my David."

"In ending, I would like to share some of our special memories with you all. Starting, of course with our map."

Behind Samantha, a photo of their world map illuminated onto a large screen. There were barely any countries untouched on the large map. The pins covered the continents, the land and the water.

"The green pins are countries we visited together. The red pins… well let's just say, the red pins are our moments." Samantha smiled a knowing smile. A secret shared just between two.

A musical chord was struck from the small chamber orchestra held at the ready beside her. Samantha took the two steps down from the podium, helped along by her son who showed her to her seat beside him in the front row. The family sat together and smiled at the library of photographic memories that played for the crowd. Laughter, interspersed with an occasional sob from a tearful mourner resonated through the chapel.

Moment after moment of joy and love played out before them. The happy snaps of Samantha, David, their children, grandchildren and great grandchildren filled the screen. Photos from countries near and far, exotic destinations, awe-inspiring adventures and smiles. Happy wide smiles from a family who obviously cared deeply.

Sebastian squeezed his mother's hand as he whispered into her ear, "That was beautiful Mum. Dad would have loved it."

"I hope so Sebastian. I truly hope I honoured him. There are truly no words to describe the loss of such a man."

"He will never be lost to you. You know that right."

Samantha nodded in agreement.

"He had to die first," Sebastian added.

"I know son. He said he couldn't bear to lose me again. This would have been what he wanted."

Sebastian leaned over and kissed his mother on the forehead, just as his father had done all those years earlier.

The music from the montage of photos began to quieten. The final images played before ending with a short piece of prose written by Samantha herself.

how is this sadness
so real it penetrates
the soul
when the longing
refuses to cease
that it grips
at my heart
the loss of you
unimaginable in my
mind
yet the wise consciousness
knows more
for it sees that
although not seen
you are never
far from reach

always in my
mind, my heart
and my soul
until I see
you again
my only
you

"Until I see you again, my David," Samantha whispered.

For their entire lives together, David and Samantha fought the battle against the mistress of time. They had known each other for most of their lives, yet even those years were still not enough to fit in everything they wanted to share together. The moments they created would be the memories they would hold on to for eternity. In those final days, every second counted as a special moment until death proved to be the ultimate timekeeper.

ACKNOWLEDGEMENTS

This publishing journey is, as always shared with family and friends, so that the end result is something I hope we can all feel a part of. I am truly honoured to have you all play an important role in the creation of these books with me.

My beautiful family, I write this story for you. To share with you and our future generations, the conversations and places that have inspired me. Without your love and support, none of this would be possible. I hope together we fill our world map with green pins.

My editor and proofreader, the grammar guru, Nadine Meyn. Your generous soul encouragers me to write and knowing that you are always there to correct my then/than is the motivation to continue to share my stories. Thank you for your hours of dedication to my work.

Elloise Sullivan, my talented graphic designer and reader. I love that you curse me when my story makes you cry and share when my continued use of the word "penis" makes you smile. I am honoured to share our creative journeys beside one another. Please let me publish your poetry!

ACKNOWLEDGEMENTS

To have both Nadine and Elloise as part of this book was beyond incredible. You are two beautiful souls that I was destined to meet.

To my two alpha readers, Melissa Spilsted and Mark Simmons. You read my stories before anyone else and challenge me to create novels that others will fall in love with. How can I ever thank you enough? (I am sure one of you will have a cheeky idea.)

Val Wiseman, my beta reader. You give great feedback, inspiration and encouragement to share the stories that come from the heart. Thank you always!

There are so many wonderful souls that support, challenge and inspire. I fear listing them all for missing out someone important. You send me photos and videos of where you enjoy the books. You share your love of my books with others. You are passionate and generous in your time and encouragement. I truly believe that sometimes things happen for a reason and we meet the people we are meant to meet. Thank you to my readers, friends, colleagues and fellow artists for all your love and support.

And finally, a thank you to my father, Mick Cox, who's family name I proudly publish under. You made me believe I could do anything and I know you are watching over and enjoying every success. I will always remember the horse temple in Hanoi which inspired this story.

222

223

224

225